Waldron Kintzing Post

Harvard stories, sketches of the undergraduate

Waldron Kintzing Post

Harvard stories, sketches of the undergraduate

ISBN/EAN: 9783743305250

Manufactured in Europe, USA, Canada, Australia, Japa

Cover: Foto ©Andreas Hilbeck / pixelio.de

Manufactured and distributed by brebook publishing software
(www.brebook.com)

Waldron Kintzing Post

Harvard stories, sketches of the undergraduate

HARVARD STORIES

SKETCHES OF THE UNDERGRADUATE

BY

WALDRON KINTZING POST

G. P. PUTNAM'S SONS

NEW YORK   LONDON
27 WEST TWENTY-THIRD STREET   24 BEDFORD STREET, STRAND

The Knickerbocker Press

1893

Electrotyped, Printed and Bound by
The Knickerbocker Press, New York
G. P. Putnam's Sons

TO

THE CLASS OF '90

CONTENTS.

PREFACE.

I CANNOT expect any one to be interested in these stories who is not interested in the scenes where they are laid. To you, my class-mates and contemporaries, I need make no apology. We always gave each other freely the valuable gift Burns asked of the gods; my shortcomings I shall learn soon enough—especially if I have written anything false or pretentious. But I feel sure that anything about Harvard, however imperfect, will not be unwelcome to you—provided it is true. We are scattered far apart and cannot often meet to talk over old times; perhaps these recollections may partially serve at times, in the place of an old chum, to bring back the days when we were all together. They are only yarns and pictures of us boys; but you will think no worse of them for that. The higher traditions of the old place I have dared in only one instance to approach.

> " The great and the good in their beautiful prime
> Through those precincts have musingly trod,"

and for that we reverence, we glory in those precincts; is it profanation to add that we also love them, because we ourselves have rollicked through them, with Jack, Ned, and Dick?

One thing, however, I must say to you before you begin to read. You will quickly see that I can claim little originality in the following stories. They are almost all founded on actual occurrences of either our own college life, or that of undergrads. before us. Some of the incidents came under my own notice, others happened to men of whom I do not even know the names, but who, I trust, will forgive my use of their experiences. But let no one imagine that, in any of the characters, he recognizes either himself or any one else. No one of us enters into these pages,—though I have tried to draw parts of all.

Among you also, my older brothers, I hope to find readers. There have been changes and developments since you were in college; many old institutions have passed away and new ones taken their places; there may be features in these sketches that you will not recognize; but

in the main, Alma Mater is still the same.
Holworthy, with all its memories, still gazes
contemplatively down the green leafy Yard;
the same old buildings flank it on either hand.
The white walls of University still look across
to the aged pair, Massachusetts and her part-
ner, the head of the family. The latter still
rears his sonorous crest (in spite of all your
historic efforts to silence it); and is it not Jones
who rings the bell? The river is there, the
elms are there; above all, the undergraduate is
there, and oh, reverend grads., from the tales I
have heard ye tell, I opine that the undergraduate is still the same. If I can recall him
to you in these sketches, if I can make one of
you say, " That is like old times," I shall have
done all that I hope.

HARVARD STORIES.

JACK RATTLETON GOES TO SPRING-
FIELD AND BACK.

THE shadow of Massachusetts had reached
across the Yard almost to University Hall,
which fact, ye who are ignorant of Harvard
topography, means that it was late in the afternoon. Hollis Holworthy was stretched in his
window seat with a book, of which, however,
he was not reading much, as his room was just
then in use as a temporary club. It was the
month of November, but Holworthy kept the
window open to let out the volume of pipe
smoke kindled by his gregarious friends. He
and his chum Rivers had an attractive room on
the Yard, up only one flight of stairs, and these
little gatherings were apt to come upon them
frequently. The eleven was going to Spring-

field next day, so the foot-ball practice on that
afternoon had been short, and several of Holworthy's "gang" who had been watching it
had dropped into the room on their way back
from Jarvis Field.   They were a typical set of
Harvard men, hailing from various and distant
parts of the nation, and of various characters;
yet all very much alike in certain respects, after
three years together around that Yard.   Rivers,
part owner of the room, who had been playing
foot-ball, came in after the rest and announced
joyfully that he had been definitely assigned
to the position of guard on the team.

"Sorry to hear it," growled Billy Bender,
who was captain of the University crew.   "You
are sure to get a bad knee or something, and
be spoiled for the boat.   I lost two good men
by foot-ball last year.   If I had my way I
would n't let any of the rowing men play the
confounded game."

"If you had your way, you old crank," said
Holworthy, "you'd strap every man in college fast to an oar.   Then you would stand
over them and crack a whip and have a bully
time.   You would have made a first-rate galley
master."

"I am tired to death of talking and hearing nothing but the game," declared Hudson. "I move to lay it on the table. There is nothing new to guess about it. I don't see how we can lose, and you don't see how we can lose, and no one sees how we can lose."

"That is apt to be the case at just this time," remarked Holworthy. "Two days from now our vision may be woefully cleared up."

"Shut up, you old croaker," cried Burleigh, throwing a sofa cushion at his host. The cushion knocked the book from Holworthy's hand and out of the window.

"You go down and get that now, you pretty, playful child," said Holworthy, indignantly. "Oh, thank you, yes, throw it up, please," he continued to someone outside. "Much obliged. No, Rattleton isn't here. I believe he went out for a ride."

"Who's that?" asked Randolph, as Holworthy drew in his head, having caught the book.

"Varnum, the coxswain."

"What the deuce does he want with Jack Rattleton?" queried Burleigh.

"I am sure I don't know," answered Holworthy, "but he and Jack are great pals, you know."

"What!" exclaimed Bender, who was not one of Rattleton's intimate friends, "Varnum and Rattleton? That is the funniest combination I ever heard of. The quietest, hardest worker in college, and the worst loafer."

"You are wrong there," said Holworthy. "If you knew Jack as well as the rest of us do, you'd know he was the best loafer in college."

"I believe that good-for-nothing chap would get up in the middle of the night to be hanged for any one of us," added Rivers.

"I am not sure about the middle of the night," said Hudson, doubtfully. "At any rate if he was to be hanged for it himself, he wouldn't get up before nine in the morning."

"How did he happen to get thick with Varnum?" inquired Bender.

"First they sat next to each other in some course," explained Holworthy. "One day Jack was out in his dog-cart, I believe, and met Varnum walking and picked him up. Jack was a Sophomore then, but a pretty good sort of a Soph., and I think he was rather surprised and interested at discovering that there were men in this University outside of his own little set, and of a new kind."

"That fellow Varnum is a rattler," said Rivers. "Hardly anyone knows him except the crew men, and, I suppose, some of his Y. M. C. A. pals. He has been making an awfully sandy fight of it, I can tell you, working his way all through college. Why, do you know, that chap came up with just two dollars and forty cents in his pocket!"

"There are lots of men doing just that sort of thing," declared Ernest Gray, a sympathetic, enthusiastic little man. "Some day we 'll be proud of having been in the same class with some of those fellows. It 's a shame that we don't know all about all of 'em."

"Oh, well," said Burleigh, consolingly, "we can always let people think we were hand in glove with the great men. 'Know him? Why he was a classmate of mine'—all that sort of thing, you know."

"Yes," said Dick Stoughton, "it 's a comfort to reflect that we can always blow about them without taking the trouble to hunt them up now."

"Awful nuisance to chase up incipient and impecunious merit," added Hudson.

"I suppose that 's why you helped Jack Rattleton take care of Varnum when he was sick. Why do you affected fools always want to cover up the precious little good you have got in you?" demanded Gray, in a mixture of sorrow and anger.

"One reason why they do it," said Holworthy, "is to make you flare up, you little powder keg. Have n't you got used to it yet, after three years?"

"Varnum is a first-rate coxswain, anyway," said Captain Bender, coming down to his regular estimate of worth. "I ran across him last year when I was looking for a light man to steer. It 's lucky I did, too; for there was a great dearth of rudder-men. This little firebrand Gray would have wrecked the 'Varsity crew to a certainty. I watched him in the class races last year—he came near grabbing stroke's oar and trying to pull himself. He nearly killed his men yelling at them in the first mile."

"I should think he did," ejaculated Randolph, who had rowed in his class crew.

"Well, we won, anyway," said Gray in defence.

"You bet we did," said Randolph, "and we tossed Gray in a blanket during the celebration just to show there was no hard feeling, and give him all the honors due to any coxswain."

"I hope Varnum won't be too busy to steer this year," said Bender. "He has a lot to do always."

While this conversation was going on in Holworthy's room, the subject of it, the man who "had a lot to do," continued on his way through the Yard. Varnum's financial struggles had not been exaggerated by Rivers. He had come up to college with almost nothing, except the clothes that he wore and a strong heart under them. He had received help at starting from the loan fund; by means of one of the numerous scholarships, tutoring, and careful economy he had succeeded in clearing his debt by his senior year. In the summer vacations he had supported himself and laid up a little money, by all sorts of employments, from that of a clerk in a country store to that of foremast hand on a yacht. Though he worked at his studies hard enough to keep the necessary scholarship, he was not a very high stand man. He was interested in some of the mission work in Boston, and gave a great deal of time to "slumming."

During the last year, too, he had made a little spare time for steering the University crew; for he found this to be a good relaxation from his work, and, besides, it brought him in contact with men whom he would not otherwise have met, many of them well worth knowing. He was not the sort of man to make friends easily, in fact he had no really intimate companion; but the man to whom he had been most attracted was one of entirely opposite character, training, and associates. His friendship with Jack Rattleton, which had been the subject of the conversation in Holworthy's room, was not an uncommon case of the attraction of extremes. Rattleton's weak nature was easily drawn to a strong one, and on the other hand "Lazy Jack Rat" was a source of amusement and interest to Varnum.

The latter once in telling Rattleton about himself had said laughingly, "My father was very much opposed to my trying to work through Harvard. He had terrible ideas about the old place; said it was a rich man's college, and if I got through it at all I should learn nothing but extravagance and evil. I have rather changed his notions now, I think; but, Rattleton, I should be afraid to show you to him, as my nearest approach to a friend."

"Why," the ingenuous Rattleton had replied, opening his mild eyes as though a little hurt as well as wondering; "I dare say I am an ass, but I don't do you any harm, do I?"

"Not a bit," answered Varnum, smiling; "on the contrary, you do me lots of good. Horrible example, you know; but if my old father ever comes to see me, don't offer to take him out in that dog-cart of yours."

"Why, it is perfectly safe," Jack had declared; "and I should be very glad to give him a drive."

As Varnum left the Yard and turned into the Square, he saw a tall thin figure approaching, astride of a diminutive polo pony, and followed by a brindled bull-terrier. Why do the men with the longest legs always ride the smallest horses, while the little men invariably perch up aloft on the tallest animal they can find? The long-legged rider put his ill-matched steed into a canter when he saw Varnum, and pulled up alongside of him.

"Hullo, Varnum," he called with a little drawl; "while I think of it, here 's that five I owe you for tutoring. Why did n't you remind me of it before."

"I have just been looking for you to dun you," answered Varnum. "I want a little cash very much just at present, so I am not going to tell you to wait until any time that is convenient."

"Fool if you did," said Jack. "No time is ever convenient with me. Somehow or other I seem to be hard up all the time. Oh, you need n't laugh. I know I have rather more to spend than most fellows out here, but that does n't help me a bit when I 've spent it. You need n't grin at this nag either, you old monk, it has n't been mine for some time. I had to give it to that robber Flynn, the livery-man, for his bill. Don't seem to have made much on the transaction, though, because now I have to hire the beast. Flynn has my horse, hang him, and somehow I 've still got his bill."

"There is no doubt about it, Rattleton," said the other; "you will be renowned as a philosopher some day. You keep discovering great truths all the time."

" Are you going to the game? " asked Rattleton, turning the subject.

" That would be a useless question to ask
most men," said Varnum; " it is equally useless to ask me. Of course I am not."

" Not?" exclaimed Jack. " Nonsense!
You 're not going to stay all by yourself here
in Cambridge? Come now, old grind, do take
a day off."

" No," said Varnum, a little sadly, shaking
his head; " I can't do it. I can't spare either
the time or the money. Besides I have something on my hands that I can't drop just at
present."

" Bet I know," said Rattleton. " It is some
of your confounded indigent kid business. Of
course, that sort of thing is bully and I admire
you for it, you know, and all that; but I should
think you might leave the indigents alone for
one day."

" Well, you see I am one myself," laughed
Varnum. " Really I can't afford it, so I don't
deserve any credit for sticking by the other
paupers."

" The special rates to Springfield are very
low," urged Jack. " I tell you what you can

do ;—just what I 'm going to do. Bet your expenses on the game and then it will all be on Yale."

"And if we lose?" queried Varnum.

"Oh, well, if we lose, we 'll only be hard up, just as we are now," was the assuring response.

"I see I have not been tutoring you in Pol. Econ. for nothing," said Varnum. "No, Rattleton, I 'd give anything I could afford to see that game, but I can't afford anything, so don't stir me up about it."

"All right, have your own way. Come 'round and dine with me to-night."

Varnum assented, and Rattleton, calling out to his dog, "come along, Blathers," rode off to the stables. On the way to his room to change his clothes he met the other men of his club table going from Holworthy's room to dinner. He told them that Varnum was coming to his table, and warned them not to talk constant foot-ball all through dinner.

"I wish I could help that chap out somehow," he said, discontentedly ; "he has got on to the tutoring dodge. He won't tutor me now, except when there is an hour exam. coming, and he knows I have got to go to somebody to be put through if I don't come to him."

On the following day the Harvard forces began to move on Springfield. The game was to be played on Saturday, but many men went on Friday afternoon, for there is great joy to be had in Springfield on the eve of battle. The Glee Club always gives a concert, after which there is a very fine ball, one of the Springfield Assemblies, I believe. There is also apt to be another ball, a " sociable " of the something-or-other coterie. Holworthy and Gray were on the Glee Club, and were going to the Assembly. The others decided to go to Springfield on that night also, and attend the other ball.

" Down with the bloated silk-stockings," declared Burleigh. " Let the kid-gloved dudes dally with the pampered aristocracy. We are the people ; we 'll go where we can turn in our waistcoats, stick our sailor-knots in our shirt fronts, and be right in the top flight ! "

The Glee Club men had rooms engaged. Hudson was on the shooting-team, and therefore also had a room secured, and the two Jacks, Rattleton and Randolph, were going on one of the club sleeping-cars. Burleigh and

Stoughton had no rooms, but were willing to take their chances of getting one.   Indeed, these two very rarely failed on an expedition of this sort in getting the best of everything. They were both sons of the energetic West, besides which Stoughton was famed for his craft, and was the recognized Ulysses of " the gang." They had a very effective method of working together in a crowd.   Ned Burleigh was six feet three, and his weight had never been accurately ascertained by his friends. Dick Stoughton, on the other hand, was of a slight and active build.   On arriving at any town where there was a rush for the hotels, Burleigh would breast the crowd with all the weight of his broad front. Stoughton, following close at his back with both the portmanteaus, would swing them, one on each side of Bur-leigh's legs, about knee high.   Thus they would cut their way through any crowd, and arriving at its front, Ned would take the baggage and come along by slow freight, while Dick dashed for the hotel.

This manœuvre was successfully executed at Springfield, and Stoughton secured the last room at the Massasoit House.

The Glee Club concert in the evening was a great success, and after it was over the respectable element, consisting of Gray and Holworthy, passed a very delightful evening at the Assembly ball. So, I grieve to record, did the low-toned members of "the gang" at the other ball. At the *soirée* of the Social Club, Ned Burleigh obtained control of the cotillion early in the evening. With Rattleton and Stoughton as right hand men, he introduced many new and pleasing figures of his own invention. In some way these three got unto themselves huge and gorgeous badges, labelled " Floor Committee," and managed the whole affair with wild success. Randolph, who came from the Sunny South, and " Colonel " Dixey, of Kentucky, picked up one or two Yale men from their section of the country, and organized an extempore Southern Club. If the governors of the Carolinas had been with them, those celebrated dignitaries, I suspect, would have experienced none of their proverbial trouble. As the evening wore on, the Southern Club, in a true brotherly spirit, extended its privileges to all the states and territories of the Union, and initiated each new member. Hudson, at first, was disconsolate, for he was on the shooting-club team that next day was to shoot a clay-pigeon match against Yale before the game. He had strict orders to go to bed early, and keep his eye clear for the next morning. At Dick Stoughton's able suggestion, however, he hunted up a member of the Yale shooting-team, and agreed to pair off with him. The excellence of this fair parliamentary procedure forcibly struck all the representative shots of both universities, except the captains. The captains of both teams at first stormed, and swore that none of their men who stayed up late or indulged in other startling innovations on the eve of battle, should be allowed to shoot on the morrow. When they found, however, that all their substitutes had "paired" also, they went off arm in arm, and were found later in a corner with a large earnest bottle between them. Altogether, as Burleigh said, "it was a very enjoyable occasion."

Next morning the clay-pigeon match came off, as usual, on the grounds of the Springfield Gun Club. It resulted in a close and glorious victory for Harvard, as the Yale team shot a little bit worse. It was a rather costly triumph, however, for both teams with their supporters drove back in a barge to the Massasoit House, and there had another meeting at the expense of the victors. Those Harvard-Yale shooting-matches are a very pleasant sport, and prolific of the best of feeling.

Before it was time to start for the battle-ground at Hampden Park, certain financial transactions took place at the hotel. The slender balance at the Cambridge National Bank, standing in the name of John Rattleton, had been wiped out on the previous day, and most of it was now deposited at the office of the Massasoit House in the joint names of J. Rattleton and a man from New Haven, to become later the sole property of one or the other. As Jack turned away from the clerk's desk, he met the steady Holworthy face to face, and looked guilty.

" Have you been betting all your quarter's income as usual, you jackass?" demanded Holworthy.

" No, only what is left of it," said Rattleton. " Might as well. If I did n't bet it, I should have to lend it all to the rest of the gang, if we get beaten. And suppose we win, as we are

2

almost sure to, and I had n't taken a blue cent
out of New Haven, and had to pay for my own
celebration; how should I feel then?" he demanded, triumphantly.

"Will you ever grow up?" asked Holworthy,
shaking his head. "Don't come running to me
if we get thrashed, that is all. I hope you have
kept your return ticket to Cambridge."

"Oh, yes, I have that," answered Rattleton,
reassuringly; "and I have twenty-five dollars
that I sha'n't put up unless I can get it up
even. These fellows want odds here, but I
think I can find even money on the field."

The Yale men are prudent bettors, however,
and Jack did not "find even money" at Hampden Park. In fact, at the last minute he could
not get a taker at any odds that even he was
willing to offer. So he kept his last twenty-
five dollars, and took his seat with his friends,
feeling that he had not done his full duty.

All the morning the trains from New Haven,
from Boston, from New York, from everywhere
within a six-hour radius, had been pouring their
heavy loads into Springfield. The north side
of Hampden Park was a crimson-dotted mass,
nearly ten thousand strong; the south side was

equally banked up with blue, and the two colors ran into each other at the ends. It is never weary waiting for the foot-ball game to begin, when the weather is good. It is amusing to see the grads come swarming to the standard. Familiar and popular faces turn up, that have been out of college only a year or two, and their owners are greeted enthusiastically by their late companions. There, too, come numbers of faces far more widely known, those of governors, congressmen, judges, architects, and clergymen. Other faces, not so conspicuous, are apparently equally interesting over the top of glowing bunches of Jacqueminots, or of violets, as the case may be. Jack Rattleton's terrier Blathers, who was rarely separated from his master on any occasion, took more interest in a big dog with a blue blanket on the other side of the field, a familiar figure at recent football games.

At about half past two o'clock a great cheer rolled simultaneously along both sides of the field, and there trotted into the lists twenty-two young specimens of this " dyspeptic, ice-water-drinking" nation. It is sometimes said that Americans are overworked and deterio-

rated from the physical standard of the race;
but as these youths of the Western branch
pulled off their sweaters and faced each other,
they did not look a very degenerate brood.
Harvard had the ball and formed a close
"wedge," Yale deployed in open line of battle.
For a moment they stood there, all crouching
forward, their heads well down, their great
limbs tense, all straining for the word to spring
at each other. There was not a sound around
the field. "Play!" called the referee, and the
Harvard wedge shot forward, and crashed with
a sound of grinding canvas into the mass of
blue-legged bodies that rushed to meet it.

For nearly three quarters of an hour the
mimic battle was fought back and forth along
the white-barred field. All the tactics of war
were there employed; the centre was pierced,
the flanks were turned, heavy columns were
instantaneously massed against any weak spot.
It was even, very even; but at last a long punt
and a fumble gave Harvard the ball, well in
the enemy's territory. A well-supported run
around the right end by Jarvis, the famous
flying half-back, two charges by Blake the terrible line-breaker, and a wedge bang through the

centre drove the ball to Yale's five-yard line. Another gain of his length by the tall Rivers. Another. Then with their backs on their very line the Yale men rallied in a way they have. Down, no gain. Now for one good push or a drop kick! Time. The first half of the game was over and neither side had scored.

"Everything is lovely," declared Hudson. "We 'll have the wind with us next half. We 've had the best of it so far, as it is. It 's a sure thing now." That was the general feeling among the Harvard supporters, and every one was happy. To the excited spectators the interval was a grateful relief, almost a necessary one to little Gray, who was nearly beside himself. He moaned every now and then over his physical inability to carry the Crimson in the lists.

After fifteen minutes' rest, the giants lined up again. The wind did seem to make a difference, for the play from the start was in Yale's ground. Jarvis the runner, who had been saved a good deal in the first half, was now used with telling effect.

Within fifteen minutes, an exchange of punts brought the ball to Yale's thirty-yard

line. After three downs Spofford dropped
back as though for a kick, and the Yale full-
back retreated for the catch. Instead of the
expected kick, Rivers the guard charged for
the left end, and the blue line concentrated on
that point to meet him, when suddenly Jarvis,
with the ball tucked under his arm, was seen
going like a whirlwind around the right, well
covered by his supports. The Yale left-end
was knocked off his legs, and the whole crimson
bank of spectators rose to its feet with a roar,
as it realized that Jarvis had circled the end.
The Yale halfs had been drawn to their right,
and every one knew that with Jarvis once past
the forwards, no one could run him down.

On he went at top speed for the longed-for
touch-line. The full-back, however, was head-
ing him off, he had outrun his interferers, and
a Yale 'Varsity full-back is not apt to miss a
clear tackle in the open. They came together
close to the line. Just as his adversary
crouched for his hips, Jarvis leaped high from
the ground, and hurled himself forward, head
first. The Yale man, like a hawk, "nailed"
him in the air, but his weight carried him on,
and they both fell with a fearful shock—over

the line! The next minute they were buried under a pile of men.

Then did all the Harvard hosts shout with a mighty shout that made the air tremble. For five minutes dignified men, old and young, cheered and hugged each other, and acted as they never do on any other occasion, except perhaps a college boat-race. The two elevens had grouped around the spot where the touch-down had been made. Suddenly the pande-monium ceased as the knot of players opened, and a limp form was carried out from among them. "It's Jarvis!" ran along the crowd, followed by an anxious murmur. A substitute ran back to the grand stand and shouted, "nothing serious, only his collar-bone." Those near the place where the plucky half-back was borne off the field could see that his face was pale, but supremely happy, and he smiled faintly as he heard the cheers of thousands, and his own name coupled with that of his Alma Mater.

The touch-down had been made almost at the corner too far aside for the try for goal to succeed. Spofford's kick was a splendid at-tempt, but the ball struck the goal post.

Then the battle began again. The Harvard team had suffered an irreparable loss in the fall of the famous Jarvis, but the score was four to nothing in its favor, and all it needed to do now was to hold its own. The Crimson was on the crest, and it was for the Blue to come up hill. Every one on the north side was elated and confident. Then began a struggle grim and great. The Yale men closed up and went in for the last chance. There was no punting for them now, the wind was against them ; but they had the heavier weight and well they used every ounce of it. Steadily, as the Old Guard trod over its slain at Waterloo, did the Blue wedge drive its way, rod by rod, towards the Harvard line. And as the fierce red Britons tore at Napoleon's devoted column, so did the Crimson warriors leap on that earth-stained phalanx. The rushers strained against it, Blake would plunge into and stagger it, Rivers and Spofford would throw their great bodies flat under the trampling feet, and bring the whole mass down over them. At last there would be a waver in the advance, three forward struggles checked and shattered, and on the fourth down, the ball would be Harvard's. On the first line up with the ball in Harvard's possession, would be heard the sound of Spofford's unerring foot against the leather and the brown oval would go curving and spinning over the heads of the rushers, far back into Yale's territory, with the Harvard ends well under it. A great " Oh ! " of relief would go up from the north side. Then those Yale bull-dogs would begin all over again. Again and again did they fight their way almost to the Harvard line, only to be driven all the way back by a long Spofford punt.

" How those Elis do fight ! " exclaimed Gray in admiration. " Don't they," admitted Burleigh ; " and is n't it nice to be able to be magnanimous and admire them ? What a lot of credit you can give a fellow when you are licking him."

" Those chaps are n't thrashed yet, my boy," said Holworthy. " They won't be, either, until the game is called, and, by Jove, they may not be then."

This observation was perfectly true. The Waterloo simile extended no further than the appearance of battle. A Yale touch-down would tie the game, and if made near the goal would probably win it. For the fourth time the New

Haven men struggled to the Cantabrigian twenty-yard line. There had been many delays in the game, and the short November afternoon had grown dark. A bad pass by the Harvard quarterback, a slip, a fumble by Spofford, might turn the result. The time was nearly up. The cheering had died almost entirely ; the excitement was too deep for that, and every one was too breathless. A short gain for Yale.

"Rattleton ? Is Mr. Rattleton here ?" called a messenger boy walking along the front of the long stand.

"Hullo, here. What 's wanted ? " answered Jack.

"Telegram for you, sir," said the boy. Rattleton did not take his eyes from the game while he tore open the envelope. Having opened it, he glanced hurriedly at the message, then jumped to his feet with a whistle. He had read :

"Come to Massachusetts General Hospital immediately when back from game.

"VARNUM."

"When does the next train leave for Boston ? " he asked the boy.

"There is one in a few minutes," was the answer.

"Whoop it up for me, children," he said to the others, "I 've got to leave. Come along, Blathers."

"Why, Jack, what 's up?"

"I don't know. Varnum wants me," and he jumped to the ground, pulling the dog after him. "The poor devil may be dying for all I know," he added to himself, as he made for the gate; "but there is no need of spoiling their fun by telling 'em."

He stretched his long legs for the station at a rate that made his four-footed chum gallop to keep up with him. The train was just starting. As he jumped aboard, he heard, from the direction of Hampden Park, the distant roar of ten thousand throats. "Hear that?" he exclaimed to the brakeman, "either the game is over or Yale has scored." Not a very enlightening conclusion.

There was a dining-car on the train, and the sight of it reminded Jack that he had had no lunch. He did not need to be reminded that he was extremely thirsty also, and actually a little worn by the afternoon's excitement. He entered the moving restaurant, and with one of his accustomed happy thoughts at such moments, was about to order an attractive lunch and a pint of champagne. Suddenly it occurred to him that if that noise had gone up from the wrong side of Hampden Park, he had just twenty-five dollars to carry him over the Christmas vacation and through January. " Furthermore," he reflected, with a knowledge born of bitter experience, " if that is the Eli yell, there won't be a mother's son in Cambridge, that I know well enough to borrow from, who will have any thing to lend,—except perhaps old father Hol. I suppose he will step into the breach as usual and pay our car-fares, but he can't support the whole gang. Hang it, I wish I was on an allowance again ; then the governor would pay my bills at Christmas and give me a blowing up. This being my own paymaster is n't what I expected when I was a Soph."

He concluded that a sandwich would support life until he got to Boston, where he could find a precarious credit. He also decided that beer was an excellent beverage, at any rate until he learned the result of the game. After this unusually prudent repast he pulled a cigar out of his pocket, and smoked it carefully in the thought that he might not have another like it for some time—at his own expense. However, he remembered consolingly that his half-colored meerschaum needed attention.

The moment Jack arrived in Boston he jumped into a herdic and drove straight to the hospital. He inquired for Varnum, and, after a little red tape had been untied, was shown into one of the public wards.

At the end of a long room on a narrow bed was Varnum, looking very white, his eyes closed. He opened them as Rattleton and the nurse approached softly, and his face seemed to light up a little when he saw Jack.

" How was the game ? " he asked, faintly.

" Splendid. Harvard four, Yale nothing," answered Jack, promptly. He did not think it worth while to mention that he had left before the end.

" Good," murmured Varnum. " Bowled over by a wagon. Awfully sorry to bring you here, Rattleton, but they thought at first I might be done for, and I don't know any one——"

" Yes, I know, old man ; cut all that," broke

in Jack. " Don't tire yourself talking. Is there anything I can do for you right away ? "

" Yes. There is a sick boy at 62 Sloven Street. Tenement house. Jimmy Haggerty. I promised to see him. There is a can of wine-jelly and a book. They must have brought them here when they picked me up. Will you take them to him and tell him that I am laid up ? It is not exactly in your line, Rattleton," he added, with a smile, " but it won't give you much trouble."

" Not a bit," declared Jack, cheerfully. " Great play for Phil. XI., you know. I can make a special report on the Sloven Street district, and it ought to pull me through the course."

" You must n't talk to him too long, sir," said the nurse.

" All right, I 'll go right off. 62 Sloven St.— Haggerty. You make yourself easy, old man, I 'll look after all your indigent kids for you, and I 'll tell the other fellows you are here. I 'll be back soon."

In answer to Rattleton's inquiries, the nurse told him how Varnum had been knocked down and run over by a runaway team in a narrow street. He had been brought to the hospital, and the doctors had at first thought his injuries fatal. Subsequent examination, however, had proved that his condition was not so serious. At his request the telegram had been sent to Rattleton. Jack left directions to have Varnum put in a private room when he could be moved, and every comfort given him. "And, by the way," he added, " don't let him know that there is any expense about it. If he objects, tell him the public wards are chuck-full ; tell him there is small-pox in 'em ; tell him any good lie that occurs to you. Send the bill to me."

The jelly and the book had not been brought in the ambulance, and no one knew anything about them. So Rattleton, stopping at the hospital office for Blathers, who had been there deposited, went first to a hotel, for all the shops were closed. From the restaurant he replaced the wine-jelly, and added some cake and a bottle of champagne. " I don't know much about what a sick boy ought to have," he thought, " but fizz is always good."

At the newspaper-stand he bought all the picture papers, and found a colored edition of nursery rhymes, which he concluded would be just the thing. "Now we are all right," he said, "come along, Blathers."

Jack had been very ready and cheerful about his mission when talking to Varnum, but he had misgivings about it as he took his way to Sloven Street, in the heart of the poorest tenement-house district. "I suppose it is easy enough just to leave this stuff and come away," he thought; "but I am sure to make some fool break." He knew there were lots of men in college who "went in for that sort of thing"; but he had had no experience of that kind himself, and Varnum was the only man he knew well, who had. He had a vague idea that Varnum held prayer-meetings among the poor, and preached as well as ministered, and he feared he might be called upon to do something of the kind himself.

It was quite dark, so he heard only one or two requests to shoot the dude, as he was passing lamp-lights, and to his infinite relief nothing was thrown at Blathers. He had expected certainly to have a row on the dog's account. In front of 62 Sloven Street he found a small boy smoking a cigarette, and inquired from him whether Jimmy Haggerty lived within.

"Sure!" assented the youngster, removing the cigarette from his lips and holding the lighted end for Blathers to smell. " Is you one o' de Ha'vards?" "Ye–es," acknowledged Jack, doubtfully, feeling that he was deceiving the little man; for he suspected that he was not exactly the kind of " a Ha'vard " that was expected in those quarters.

"Well say, how did de game come out? I ain't seen de bulletin-boards."

Jack's heart leaped towards the boy at once; he discovered that there was a bond of sympathy between them after all.

"I don't know," he answered; "I came away before the end. It was four to nothing in our favor then."

"Chamesy Haggerty lives on de tird floor. I 'll show ye up." Jack followed his pilot up the dark, smelly stairs, answering questions all the way as to the foot-ball game.

" A–ah, ye can't do notin' widout Jarvis," commented the youngster, upon hearing of the half-back's injury.

" Dat 's a nice lookin' purp yer got," he said, eyeing Blathers, as they arrived at the third floor. " Guess he 's a good 'un to fight, ain't he?

Le 'me take care of him for yer, while you 're inside."

Jack did not accept this kind offer. His guide, pointing to a door, said : " Well, dat 's Chimmie's. I ain't goin' in, 'cause he 's got scarlet fever."

" The devil he has ! " exclaimed Jack.

" Yare ; leastways dat 's what dey all say. Wait till I get down-stairs 'fore yer open de door.". And with a vain whistle to Blathers he disappeared down-stairs.

Rattleton knocked at the door indicated as " Chimmie's," and opened it in response to a voice within. The small room was pretty well lighted by a lamp, the first thing that Jack's eye fell on. It was Varnum's student-lamp; Jack knew it at once from a caricature he had himself drawn on the shade. A hard-faced, slovenly old woman was sitting near a stove, and looked at him in surprise as he entered.

" Is this Mrs. Haggerty ? " he asked.

" I am," she answered; "what do you want ? "

" Mr. Varnum sent these things," replied Rattleton. " He could n't come himself because he has been hurt, and is in the hospital."

"Is that so? Sure, I'm sorry to hear that," said the woman with real regret in her tone. "Mr. Varnum has been kind to us, I tell you. He's helped me with my boy Jimmy here ever since he's been sick."

"Dat's too bad," complained a thin voice from the corner. On the other side of the lamp was a bed, from under the dirty quilt of which protruded a little pale face. "Ain't he coming to read to me? What's de matter wid him?"

Jack explained, with an accompaniment of sympathetic "tut-tuts" from the woman and more forcible expressions from the sick boy.

"I'm obliged to him for the things," said the former, as Rattleton handed her his burden. She looked at the bottle with a puzzled and half-frightened air.

"That's the first time ever Mr. Varnum give us anythin' like that. The poor young feller must be dizzed, by the hurt of him. I'll hide that." And to Rattleton's horror she shoved the bottle of Irroy under the stove.

"Would you do me a bit of a favor, sir," she asked, "like Mr. Varnum would do?"

"With pleasure,—that is if I can," answered Jack, cautiously, wondering what she wanted, and with a dread that it might be in the nature of religious services.

"I got to go out to see the doctor, and I 'd take it friendly would you sit wid th' boy, till I get back. I 'll not be long."

"Why, yes, of course," said Rattleton, feeling how much worse it might have been.

The woman took down her shawl, and throwing it over her head, drew out the bottle she had just hidden, and tucked it under her arm out of sight. "I 'll ask the doctor whether this is good for the kid," she muttered. "If Jamsey don't need it, I can sell it. I know some one else it ain't good for."

Opening the door she first looked out cautiously, then hurried down-stairs.

"Wonder what I ought to do now?" thought Rattleton. Blathers was over at the bed making friends with the patient.

"Dis your dog? nice one, ain't he. Is you one o' de student fellers?"

Jack admitted that he was, knowing that the word "student" was used in its generic, not its strict sense.

"You 're a friend o' Mr. Varnum's, eh? He 's nice, ain't he?"

Rattleton agreed emphatically that Varnum *was* "nice."

"Yare," continued the boy, "he 's a daisy. He comes in and reads to me all de time. Mr. Talcot, he comes too sometimes; but he ain't as nice as Mr. Varnum. Hullo, you been to de game?"

This last question was elicited by the sight of the little bit of crimson ribbon stuck through Rattleton's buttonhole,—an *insignium* brought from the seat of war. In cheerful compliance with the demand to hear all about it, Jack sat down by the bed, and recounted, as well as he could, all the details of the afternoon's battle. He described Jarvis' splendid run, and how he had scored and at the same time broken his collar-bone in his great plunge for Harvard and glory. As he told of it he thought of Varnum lying alone in the hospital.

"Would you like me to read to you?" suggested Jack, when the foot-ball subject had been exhausted.

"You bet," assented the patient. "I ain't heard no readin' all day. Mudder can't read, and Sis ain't been here."

"Here 's a book I brought," said Rattleton,

picking up the bright-pictured nursery rhymes. "I don't know whether it 's interesting," he added, doubtfully.

For a little while he read the classics of *Mother Goose* in his gentle drawl, until the boy interrupted him.

"Say, what sort o' baby's stuff is dat, anyhow? I don't t'ink much o' dat. I 'd sooner hear *Dare-Devil Dick* dan dat."

"I am inclined to agree with you," replied Rattleton. "Really, you see, I had n't read this for so long that I had forgotten just what it was like. Let 's have *Dare-Devil Dick.*"

"I ain't got it now. I give it away. Mr. Varnum, he gi' me a book he said was better, and I guess it is. It 's got an A-1 scrapper in it, too, dat could do Dare-Devil Dick wid one hand. He did n't kill so many people, but I t'ink he was a better feller. 'Dere it is at de foot o' de bed."

Rattleton took up the book indicated. It was *Westward Ho!* He sat down again by the bed, and opened the book at a place where there was a mark. Then the two went out from the little squalid room, and sailed away over the Spanish Main with tall Amyas Leigh and his good men of Devon. For over half an hour the little invalid street-arab and the hare-brained Harvardian were both wrapped in the spell of the apostle to the Anglo-Saxon youths.

Before Rattleton had finished reading he heard the door open and close, and a rustle of skirts. Looking up he saw, not the old woman, but a rather gaudily-dressed young one. Jack thought he had seen her face before some-where. That was quite possible, I regret to say.

" Hullo, Sis," said the boy. " Me sister," he explained to Rattleton. The young woman looked with surprise at the latter, as he rose to his feet. Her eye glanced at his stick and his bull terrier, and all over his clothes, from his shoes up ; then narrowly scrutinized the face of the thoroughly uncomfortable youth. Though the shyest of men, this was the first time he had ever felt very bashful in such a presence. Then she asked, disdainfully, " What 's one o' your kind doing here ? "

Jack colored to his hair. " I—I don't know exactly, myself," he stammered. " You see I came to take the place of my friend who is ill," he explained, apologetically.

" I know you now," said the girl, her look softening a little. " You 're the sport that done up Dutch Jake for kickin' a kid one night in Stuber's restaurant."

" I *have* been in there occasionally," Jack confessed. He was going to add " I am sorry to say," but remembered that might be rude. " I promised Mrs.—er—Mrs. Haggerty, to sit here until she returned," he continued, " but I suppose I am not needed now ? "

" No, much obliged to you, I 'll stay with Jimmy till she gets back."

Jack took up his hat and stick, but paused a moment awkwardly as he turned to leave.

" Would you—er—would you mind," he said, hesitatingly, " my — er — my— er — my *lending* a little money—for the boy, you know ? "

The girl laughed bitterly. " I guess we can stand it," she said. " If you never spent your money worse than that, I 'm mistaken. You can give us the tin. We ain't proud."

" Thanks," murmured Jack, vaguely feeling that he was being helped out of an awkward attempt. He pulled out the contents of his pocket, both bills and change. " I dare say you *will* spend it better than I."

Just as he was handing the money to the girl, there was a knock on the door, and in answer to her heedless " come in " a man entered. It was a classmate, named Talcot, whom Jack knew only by sight as one of Varnum's " Y. M. C. A. pals." He stopped in astonishment, and then frowned, as he recognized Rattleton, and saw him giving the money.

" Mr. Rattleton, I believe ? "

Jack looked him in the eye, and nodded stiffly.

" Don't you think, sir," asked the worthy student, with an indignant sneer, " that you had better confine yourself to your expensive clubs, and to your regular haunts in town ? "

Jack colored again, the shade of his little ribbon ; but this time it was not a blush. He bit his lip for a moment, and gripped his stick hard.

" I am afraid I had," he said very slowly, as he moved towards the door. " But I will tell you one thing, Mr. Talcot," he added as he paused in the doorway. "I am an awful fool, I know, but I am not mean enough to think that every damn fool must be a damn rascal. I will give you an opportunity later to apologize. Good-night, Jimmy. Come along, Blathers," and he strode down-stairs.

" Pheugh," puffed Rattleton, as he got out in the grateful fresh air again. " I got it in the neck twice in that round. Guess I 'd better keep out of that kind of a ring hereafter."

He went back to the hospital, and found that Varnum was asleep, and resting comfortably. " Now, by Jove, Blathers, we 'll have dinner!" he exclaimed, joyfully, as he left the hospital. " I 'm nearly dead," he thought, " we 'll go to the Victoria and have a bang-up din, and a bot— No we won't, either," he suddenly concluded, as he thrust his hands into his pockets, " we 'll go to Billy Parks." He had a bill at Park's. There was also a fair prospect of his walking out to Cambridge that night, unless he met a friend ; for he had forgotten to keep even a car-fare. Holworthy always declared that Rattleton would forget his head some day, and Jack now expressed a fear of that nature himself, when he discovered the void in his pockets.

Annoyance never chummed long with Jack Rattleton, however, and it had left him by the time he got to Park's restaurant. He looked over the bill-of-fare with the delight of anticipation and expended a good deal of careful thought in his selection.

"Let 's see, shall I fool with Little Neck clams? Yes, I can have those while they are cooking the rest. Mock turtle soup, and then filets of sole ; they are mock, too, but they are very good. Then bring me some of that chicken pasty. Yes, you can call it *vol-au-vent* if you like, but don't stick me extra for the name; I would just as lief eat it in English. Then I want half a black duck. Tell the cook it is for me, and I don't want coot. After that I 'll decide as to the next course. Bring me a half bottle of Mumm, and a long glass with chopped ice in it, and bring that right away. Oh! by the way," he called, as the waiter was starting off with the order, " find out at the desk how the game came out. Gad, I 'd nearly forgotten it ! "

" Why, sir," replied the waiter, " have n't you

heard? Too bad. Six to four. Yale made a touch-down in the last five minutes, and kicked a goal from it."

"Wha–at!" exclaimed Jack. "Hi! waiter! Hold on a minute; come back here! Make that order one English chop and a mug of musty."

THE WAKING NIGHTMARE OF HOLLIS
HOLWORTHY.

HOLWORTHY had accepted an invitation to dine at the Tremonts' in Boston. There was nothing remarkable about that ; but so had Jack Rattleton, and that *was* remarkable. He had done so chiefly on Holworthy's account. He rarely went anywhere in Boston society, as he held that to do so was a waste of precious time given to him for a college education. He could employ his evenings much better in Cambridge in his study, with a select party, or in one of the clubs. True, he often went over the bridge ; but that, as he said, was always with some earnest purpose, such as a study of the drama at the Howard Athenæum, or to attend a benefit of Prof. Murphy or some other revered instructor. He never frittered away his moments in the vapidity of a polite ballroom. Dinners he especially abhorred (except, of course, serious masculine dinners); chiefly because dinner engagements had to be kept, and worse, kept punctually. For that reason they were, in Jack's estimation, as bad as lectures to a man on probation. He had decided to bind himself to this dinner, however, because he knew the Tremonts very well, and happened to know they were going to invite Holworthy, and also happened to know that some one else was going to be there about whom Holworthy did not like to be chaffed. He foresaw a possible opportunity of " seeing Hol do the devoted and breaking him up "; so for this benevolent purpose he determined to sacrifice himself.

Now, Holworthy knew naught of this, and when Rattleton casually mentioned to him that he (Jack) had been bidden to a dinner at the Tremonts', and asked him for the most approved form for a lying regret, he used all his powers of persuasion to make Rattleton accept. He preached a sermon on the evil effects of Jack's Bohemian ways and neglected opportunities. He said he was going to that same dinner and would bring Jack back in a cab. Finally, after much objection, and after getting as many bribes out of his mentor as possible, Rattleton agreed to go, and also agreed to do his best not to be late.

On this latter point Hollis spent half an hour. He insisted, and impressed upon Jack in every way, that a man could do nothing more outrageous than to keep his hostess waiting for him for dinner. Holworthy, it may be observed, had been brought up with old-fashioned ideas of good breeding. His father had taught him never to fail, or be late at a dinner or a duel, if once engaged for either. He cautioned Rattleton not to put his faith in excuses, for they were always weak and as naught. " Everybody," said he, " knows you are lying, and you know that they know you are lying, and they know that you know that they know you are lying."

" That 's so," acknowledged Jack, with a melancholy shake of his head. " At one time, when I went in for these vanities, I used to have some pretty good excuses, but they are all played out now. I have broken down every cab in Cambridge, given every horse the blind staggers, and ruined the reputation for sobriety of every driver. I have broken my own leg once or twice, and limped painfully into the room ; that was very effective, until I once favored the wrong leg. The electric cars were

a great help when they first came in, but I
have long since dislocated every trolly on
the line."

"Well, above all," said Holworthy, "if you
should happen to be late, don't try that worn out
chestnut about the drawbridge being open, as
I heard a poor young Freshman do the other
night, with a happy confidence."

"Do you take *me* for a Freshman?" responded Jack, indignantly. "At the first dinner
I went to when I first came up, I started to use
the drawbridge, and the old grad. with whom I
was dining took the words out of my mouth
and then laughed at me."

"The best thing for you to do," suggested
Hollis, as his final advice, "is to get a chain
and make yourself fast to your bedstead from
now until the evening of the dinner. I'll come
round and unchain you when it is time to dress.
At any rate, I shall endeavor to keep you in
sight all that day." All of which Rattleton
took humbly, and promised to do his best.

But on the afternoon of the appointed day
Jack was not to be found. Holworthy hunted
in vain for him at all his usual haunts, and in
the evening began dressing himself with many

misgivings. While he was still in his room, his chum Charles Rivers came in from the afternoon's work in the University boat. Holworthy complained to him of the way in which the man Rattleton was turning his hair gray.

"Looking for Lazy Jack, are you?" laughed Rivers, reassuringly; "well, he was in a four-oar above the Brighton Abattoir not very long ago. I could n't see him, because I had to keep my eyes in the boat, but I could hear him objurgating Steve Hudson for hitting up the stroke. We passed them as we were pulling back from Watertown. It was n't half an hour ago."

Holworthy made a short remark about Rattleton that has nothing to do with the story. "I have only just time to get into the Tremonts' now," said he, as he threw on his cloak, "but I will stop at the shiftless beggar's room before I go in. He may possibly have got back and dressed."

He hurried along Harvard Street, and on the corner ran into a lot of men coming up from the river. Sauntering along in their flannels, perfectly happy after the glorious exercise and bath, he saw Hudson, Randolph, Stoughton,—

4

and the long form of Mr. Rattleton, quite as usual, hands in his pockets, head thrown back, a smile on his face, content in his soul, and nothing on his mind. There was a sudden change in his aspect, however, when he caught sight of Holworthy's silk hat and white tie. He stopped, aghast, with a " By Jove!" and then, " Oh, the devil!"

"Yes," exclaimed Holworthy, hotly, "and that is just where you will go some day from sheer carelessness. That is the one appointment you 'll keep,—though, I believe, you will be late for your own funeral."

"Don't wait for me, old man. I 'll be there as soon as I can," answered Jack, ambiguously.

"Wait for you!" Hollis cried, " I wash my hands of you! If you choose to disgrace yourself, it is none of my business. As it is now, I may be late myself," and he boarded a car for Boston.

Now it was so that Holworthy did not know the Tremonts. They were old friends of his family, and he ought to have called on them when he first came to college ; but he had not, and they had been abroad since his Freshman year. He was not even perfectly certain of where they lived, and he had forgotten, in his hurry on leaving his room, to look at the address on the invitation ! He thought of this fact when he was over the bridge and well into Boston. However, he pretty clearly remembered having sent his acceptance to 142 Marconwealth Street. It was either 142 or 242 ; but to make sure he decided to look it up in a Blue Book. He, therefore, got out at Park Square and went into a druggist's, to consult the little directory.

He first looked up 142 Marconwealth Street, and found the name of Jones. Then he looked for 242, 342, 442,—he felt there was a 42 in the combination somehow,—but all were vacant of Tremonts. He tried the 42's of other streets, but in vain. Then, in desperation, he ran down the whole list of Tremonts. Reader, dost thou know aught of the ancient town of Boston ? If not, look some time into a Boston Blue Book, open anywhere, and see what Holworthy saw. In Boston, when they want to describe a particularly luxuriant forest, they say that its leaves are as the Tremonts. Hollis was not even sure of the first name of his intended host ; he thought it was Mayflor.

There were three Mayflor Tremonts on Marconwealth Street, one at each end and one in the
middle.   Of other Tremonts on that street
there were fourteen.

The cold sweat stood on Holworthy's brow
in the most approved style.   It was already
half past seven, the hour of dinner, for he had
spent several minutes in his Blue Book research.   Only one plan occurred to him.   He
bought the book at an extravagant price and
jumped into a cab, determined to hunt down
that dinner if he had to go to every Tremont
in Boston.   He began with the Mayflor
Tremonts.   When the servant answered the
bell, he would ask if there was a dinner-party
going on in that house.   He was not sure
whether he was taken for a lunatic or a society
reporter, but did not care which.   None of the
Mayflor Tremonts were giving dinners on that
evening.   Then he began at one end of Marconwealth Street, and tried every Tremont
in order.

All this time the minutes were joining the
past eternity, and he, Hollis Holworthy, was
getting later and later for dinner.   At the sixth
house, however, as a maid opened the door, he

heard the sounds of gentle revelry and small
talk, and his heart leaped for joy.   The maid
said, "Yes, we have a party here to-night."
He rushed back and paid for his cab, not stopping for the paltry change due him, amounting
to half that he gave.   He left his coat and hat
in the hall to save time and, without asking
further questions, strode by the maid into the
dining-room.   He was twenty-five minutes late,
and glad they had not waited for him.

Going up to the hostess, he began, "Mrs.
Tremont, I can't tell you how mortified—" the
table was filled!   There was no vacant chair!
Then he noticed that the hostess was looking
a little blank, though smiling and polite.   "I
beg your pardon," he said, as his heart sank,
"have I made some awful mistake?   My name
is Holworthy; did you not invite me to dinner
this evening, or have I got the wrong house?
—or the wrong night?

"I am afraid you *have* made a mistake, Mr.
Holworthy," replied the lady, "and I think it
must be in the house."

"Well, can you tell me," asked the blushing
and desperate youth, trying to keep a groan
out of his question, "whether you happen to

know of any other Mrs. Tremont who is giving a dinner to-night? I have lost the address, and I am dinnerless in the streets of Boston."

The hostess laughed a little at Holworthy's despair, but relieved him by saying that her cousin, Mrs. Mayflor Tremont, had said something that day about a dinner.

" But I have been to the houses of three Mrs. Mayflor Tremonts on this street," protested poor Hollis. " Is there another one?"

" Why, Hol," spoke up Ernest Gray, an intimate friend, who was present to Holworthy's great comfort, "that is where Jack Rattleton told me that you and he were going—the Mayflor Tremont's, 142 Marconwealth Street."

"That is just what I thought," said Holworthy, " but the Blue Book gives one Jones at 142."

" Oh!" explained Mrs. Tremont, " they have only just moved in, and their name has not been changed in the Blue Book."

" Then *that* was my ruin," Hollis exclaimed. "Thank you very much, indeed. I hope you will forgive me for making such a scene," and he retreated with as much dignity and haste as could be combined. He was too much relieved to mind Gray's remark, "That is one on you, Hol," or the laugh that he heard as he got to the front door.

His cab had only moved to the corner, and he hailed it again. The driver repaid his recent generosity by getting him to 142 in less than three minutes.

Let us now see how it fared with Jack, the grasshopper. At the moment when Holworthy took the car in Harvard Square, there was seen a rare phenomenon of nature;—Rattleton showed acute animation. He went up Harvard Street with two leaps to a block. Riley's cab, as usual, was standing at the corner of Holyoke Street, and as Jack dashed by, he yelled for Riley. The latter came tumbling out of Foster's, and, in forty-three seconds and two fifths, had his chariot at the door of Rattleton's staircase. Both Riley and his horse are as well drilled to emergencies as are the men and steeds of a fire-engine. Jack reached his room in record time, and only stopped to wash his face and hands. He grabbed his evening clothes and shoes, a "boiled" shirt and tie, and was in the cab almost as soon as it got to the door.

"Riley," said he, "get me to 142 Marcon-wealth Street before Mr. Holworthy, and I 'll try and pay what I owe you this week. It is a matter of life and death, and I expect you this day to do your duty. Don't be beaten by an electric car."

The latter part of this exhortation had its effect. Riley follows the Golden Rule and never duns anybody, but his weak spots are his professional pride and his sporting blood. Touch him there, and you will travel in his cab as in the car of Phœbus. He has never lost the day when it was possible for man and horse to save it. Ned Burleigh used to say that he would back Riley's nag against Salvator, provided the former should have behind him the cab, Riley, and a load. On this particular occasion he fully maintained his reputation.

While rushing towards Boston, Rattleton proceeded to dress. He at first complimented himself on not having forgotten anything; but, when he came to his shirt, behold, there were no studs! He had been wearing a soft cheviot, and had only a collar button. The absence of sleeve buttons would probably not be noticed, but he could not go to dinner with a studless chest. For a minute he thought the game was up, wrecked by such a little thing. Then an inspiration came to him. With his knife he cut three little pearl buttons out of his undershirt, leaving a piece attached to each button. These he pushed through his shirt, and they were held in place by the pieces of flannel at their backs. It had always been suspected by his friends that Jack Rattleton really had brains, though he never made the exertion to use them. It had even been said that some time in an emergency he might show positive genius. He looked at those improvised studs with satisfaction, as he reasoned to himself that they would be taken for imitation buttons and, therefore, go unnoticed. If they should be recognized as real, that would be all the better; it would look like a new fashion, and one of most "swagger" simplicity. He tied his cravat all right by feeling; but he had not thought of a hair-brush, and his hair was all damp and on end after his shower-bath at the boat-house. This did not trouble him, however, as he was sure of finding a brush at the Tremonts, in the room where the men would leave their coats.

He had hardly finished this flying toilet when he arrived at the house, not two minutes late. He instructed Riley to come back at ten, and that the return trip would be "on Mr. Holworthy." In the dressing-room there were hair-brushes, as he had expected, and he went down to the drawing-room in faultless order, feeling that he had made a great discovery. Undoubtedly a cab was just the place for a hurried man of business, like himself, to dress.

He called the attention of his hostess to his punctuality, and assured her that such a thing in him was a sign of the greatest devotion. "You see," said he, "when I am late, everyone says, 'Oh, it is only that shiftless Jack Rattleton,' and when I am on time, I want the credit for it. Now it is nothing particularly praiseworthy for a man like Holworthy to be on time. If he should ever slip up, it might well be put down as an insult, because he never forgets or dawdles. Some day his good reputation will be the ruin of him. I think my system is the better." After which airy persiflage, Rattleton noticed that Holworthy was not in the room ; and ten minutes later, when the latter was still absent, he began to wish he had let airy persiflage alone. Everybody else had arrived. Five minutes more went by, and when twenty minutes were gone and no Holworthy, Jack went to Mrs. Tremont and told her how Hollis had left Cambridge in plenty of time, and, in fact, had refused to wait for him. "Something must have happened to him," he said, rather anxiously, " and I am prepared to back up as strictly true any excuse he may offer, for I can swear he left Cambridge more than an hour ago, and was coming right here."

"No accident to himself, I hope," replied Mrs. Tremont. "At any rate, I think we had better go in, as I am sure Mr. Holworthy will feel more comfortable if we do not wait for him."

So in they went, Rattleton taking her whom Holworthy should have taken, for Jack was one of two extra men.

And Hollis, where was he? Suffering in the cab.

Ten minutes later, as he went up the stoop of 142, an insidious policy stole into Holworthy's brain. He had lost the invitation and mistaken the number of the house,—why should

he not have mistaken instead the hour of
dinner? Was that not better than to be
ignorant of the address of his hostess, upon
whom he ought to have called long before
this? He was in good time for an eight
o'clock dinner, and most dinners are at eight
nowadays. Then, too, Rattleton would be
just about half an hour late, and would probably be utterly unconcerned about it, and offer
no excuses. That would lend color to a suspicion that Mrs. Tremont had herself made
the mistake, in writing some of the invitations.
He would not need to tell any actual untruth
—to say distinctly that he thought dinner was
at eight. He need only imply it, and apologize for his evident mistake. It would be a
pretty poor plea for a very bad crime, but at
any rate it was a more polite explanation than
the real one, and less ridiculous. Oh, Hollis
Holworthy, that thou shouldst thus forget the
veritas, the watchword of thine Alma Mater!

In the dressing-room was a straw hat with a
colored ribbon. "Hullo," he surmised, "Jack
is here. Wonder if the rest of his outfit corre-
sponds, and he has come in his blazer." As
he went into the dining-room, his eye first

lighted on that interesting person whom Mr. Davis has capitally termed "A Girl He Knew." On her right was Rattleton, on her left a vacant chair. She must have had to go in alone!

With a look of gentle surprise and concern, that, he flattered himself, was rather well done, he went up and saluted Mrs. Tremont.

"Have I been mistaken," he asked, "in thinking that dinner was at eight o'clock, or has my watch betrayed me?" There was no fib in this and what could be more diplomatic?

Mrs. Tremont stood it for a second, then she happened to catch sight of Rattleton's face. It was too much for her, and she burst out laughing. After all, it was the best thing to do.

"Now, Mr. Holworthy, tell us what really happened, and we will believe and forgive you. Jack, here, has testified to the time of your departure from Cambridge, and you must fill in the interim somehow."

Then Hollis made a clean breast of the whole thing, and made the tale of his sufferings as moving as possible, finishing with a request for some dust to put on his head. He was so humble that even Rattleton was sorry for him; but the memory of many of Holworthy's lectures came to Jack and he could not resist suggesting to Mrs. Tremont, as Hollis took his seat, that as Holly's blood had run so cold she ought to have some soup warmed up for him.

That evening, on the way back to Cambridge in the cab, was spent one of the pleasantest half hours of Rattleton's life. He told Holworthy how a man could do nothing more outrageous than to keep his hostess waiting for dinner. He said he had a very good chain that he used for his dog Blathers, but which he could lend Hollis. He warned him some day that he would surely go to the devil by his careless habits. "Above all," said he, "never put your faith in excuses. Everybody knows you are lying, and even if you don't know that they know, etc., you sometimes find out."

Holworthy smoked his cigar vigorously without saying a word in reply. When they arrived at their club in Cambridge he asked, resignedly: "Well, what do you want for supper?"

"I know I ought to take champagne," answered Jack, graciously, "but as you are so very humble and I don't really want any more fizz, I will let you off with a rarebit and beer. But don't you ever jump on me again."

THE PLOT AGAINST BULLAM.

SOMETHING had to be done about the case of Sergeant Bullam. For years he had ruled his beat with a rod of iron. Many a noble spirit had fallen a prey to his desire for notoriety and promotion. The slightest offence, the most innocent or technical infringement of the law, was sufficient pretext for him to indulge his thirst for student incarceration. The *lettres de cachet* and the Bastile were nothing to Bullam and the Cambridge jail. In the dark days when the ungrateful University town went prohibition, the tyrant had revelled in his opportunities. He had raided several of the club-houses and had charged Hollis Holworthy, the president of one of the clubs, with keeping a liquor nuisance. Of course this little joke on the superb Holworthy had exceedingly pleased all his friends ; but it did not excuse Bullam. There had been isolated attempts at resistance and vengeance, and these had sometimes been successful, but never yet had Bullam suffered any great public downfall worthy of his oppression. He was wary to a high degree, and never ventured into the sacred Yard, where his uniform would have been only blue cloth and his buttons common brass.

The crafty Stoughton, however, had a scheme. He had been pondering over the case for some time, and Dick rarely pondered for nothing. He was known to his intimates as Machiavelli, called Mac the Dago for short. This particular plan was indeed worthy of his great namesake. He imparted it to Jack Randolph, who had the heaviest personal score against Bullam, and, therefore, the best title to share in his humiliation. They fixed the following night as Bullam's Ides and announced it to all their friends. They posted it in all the clubs, and in every way spread the glad tidings that on the morrow Bullam should be utterly cast down. They fixed the hour at about ten o'clock in the evening, and exhorted the people to gather themselves together in a great concourse to see their enemy made a cause of laughter unto them. The promise of the avenging prophets was to conduct a triumph along the whole length of

Harvard Street and to lead in their train the haughty Bullam, humbled and a captive; he should even act as their body-guard if they so chose, and prevent all interference by his brothers of the force. How this millennial spectacle was to be brought about, they kept carefully secret.

There is, perhaps, in every man a certain element of moral obliquity, which, as he is put through any civilizing process, is squeezed out of him from time to time in varying forms and quantities. It comes to the surface, makes itself acutely felt and apparent for a short time, and then drops off,—just as a physical poison would act in his veins. At any rate, this is the only theory that can explain the highly reprehensible but firmly established custom among Harvard Freshmen of "ragging" signs. "Ragging," uninitiated reader, simply means stealing. What amusement, profit, or glory the Freshman finds in it has never been ascertained. He cannot tell exactly himself, and, as soon as he ceases to be a Freshman, wonders why he ever indulged in the habit. Perhaps the charm lies in the chance of getting into a scrape; but in most instances a sign can be taken with perfect safety.

Now I cannot possibly think why I—but that is another story, as Mr. Kipling says.

I am going to digress, however, for one story in this connection. Ned Burleigh used to tell it on his room-mate, Steve Hudson. Steve always denied it vehemently, and declared that Burleigh did not even deserve the credit of a fabricator; that the story had been in college for years, and he had heard it told by a '42 man. Ned held that made no difference; that some one had to carry it for our four years and Steve was the best man for the position. According to him, Hudson, in walking back from Boston on a dark night in Freshman year, spied a tempting sign hanging on a door-post. He secured it by some difficult climbing, and tucking it under his overcoat, went on his way. On arriving in his room he announced that he had a prize, and, unbuttoning his coat, he displayed to Burleigh's delighted gaze, his only evening suit and the sign " Fresh Paint."

This practice of stealing signs had made Bullam's meat of many a Freshman. In fact, the diligent Sergeant depended upon it for most of his κυδος, so Dick Stoughton had determined to play upon his keenness in this

respect, and use a sign as the bait with which
to hook his fish.   On the appointed evening he
and Randolph went to Cambridgeport, and
bought a barber's pole.   They were careful to
get a receipted bill from the barber with an
accurate description of the pole.   The latter
was marked with the barber's name in gilt
letters, and was small enough to be nearly, but
not quite, covered with an overcoat.   Thus
provided, they started back for Cambridge
proper (the Port being usually known as Cambridge improper) along Main Street, keeping as
much as possible in the shadows.   At the end
of half a dozen blocks, they came on a policeman, and promptly crossed the street in a most
alluring manner.   The vigilant officer, noticing
the suspicious shape of Randolph's overcoat
held under his arm, gave chase.   The end of
the pole stuck out from the coat, and it was
useless for the students to protest that they had
nothing that did not belong to them.   They
assured their captor that the pole was theirs,
that they had paid for it and could prove the
fact ; but he insisted upon taking them before
the captain of the precinct.

The captain had had a hard day, and was

preparing to go to bed when they were brought before him. He was tired and cross, and his humor was not improved by this new arrival. When Stoughton showed the receipt, however, he at once discharged the prisoners with much pleasure, and reprimanded the overcareful officer.

The two then went on to the next guardian of Main Street, and he bit equally well. They warned him of the result, and gave him their word of honor that the pole was not stolen. He hesitated, and for a moment they feared that he was going to be decent enough to believe them. But he was a new and zealous recruit on the force and the bait was too inviting; so he decided not to trust them. He was as polite as possible about it and when he even apologized for not taking their word, they came near melting and showing the receipt, But the fall of Bullam was not to be averted, simply because gentler tyrants might be entrained. So back they went to headquarters.

The captain came down in a red dressing-gown, the skirt of which flapped idly in the breeze that came through an open window in the office. His bare feet were shoved into a pair of carpet slippers, each foot in the wrong slipper. With one hand he held a candle that wiggled in the candle-stick and dropped wax on his wrist, and with the other hand tried to keep the dressing-gown about his person. His frame of mind faithfully carried out the spirit of the picture. To any guilty prisoner he would have been indeed a terrifying spectacle; but he could do nothing to the innocent and insulted gentlemen who had been haled before him. He therefore relieved himself on their captor. The poor man got such a dressing down, that when they left the office, Randolph presented him with full forgiveness, a dollar bill, and the advice to learn as soon as possible to tell a Senior from a Freshman.

The next policeman they met was old George Smith. He held them up with a look of surprise, and a remark that he thought they had been in college too long to be " ragging " barber's poles. When they explained to him, however, he of course believed them, and grinned as he perceived something in the wind.

" It is lucky that was George," said Stoughton, as they went on. " If we had struck a strange cop, who thought we were liars, we should have brought down the wrong bird. That police captain is just exactly primed and loaded to the muzzle, and all ready to go off. Now for Bullam!"

They had now reached Quincy Square, and saw the fated form of Bullam loom in the offing. They made for him boldly ; there was no need of finessing in his case. The moment his hawk eye caught sight of the ill-concealed pole, he bore down on them with a grim joy.

" What have you got under that coat ? " he demanded in his usual suave tone.

" None of your business," responded Jack Randolph, with an inward chuckle.

" It is n't, eh ! Do you think I can't see that pole a-sticking out there ? Do you think you can steal signs under my very nose? You come along with me now, and we 'll see whether it 's none of my business."

" If your insulting remarks refer to this barber-pole," replied Randolph, producing the pole with ostentatious confidence, " allow me to tell you that it belongs to us, and we have a perfect right to carry it wherever we please. Although, as I said before, it is none of your business, I will condescend to let you know that I bought it lately, and have a receipt for it in my pocket."

"You can't give me no such bluff as that," sneered Bullam. "You can tell that to the captain of the precinct. I 'll give you a chance to show your receipt."

"Look here, my man," (nothing makes a gentleman of Bullam's class more angry than to call him " my man ") answered Stoughton, "you don't deserve it after the language you have used to us, but, nevertheless, I give you fair warning not to do anything of the kind. If you take us to the captain, you will get into trouble."

Bullam was beside himself. The more they said to him the more furious he became, and finally threatened to use his club " if they gave him any more guff." So, in high delight, the two injured youths took their way a third time towards the house of the captain.

The policeman who had last had them in charge turned quickly away as they passed, and shoved his handkerchief into his mouth. It was a grateful balm to the new man to see a veteran going into the same trap that had just lacerated him. Moreover, Bullam was quite as unpopular in the force as with the students.

All was dark in the house where lay the uneasy head that wore the crown of the precinct. Bullam rang the bell, with a ferocious glare at his prisoners, as though tolling their death knell. A minute afterwards a window opened above, and a head was thrust forth.

" Who is there?" bellowed a voice, now familiar to our much-arrested pair.

" Sergeant Bullam, sir, with an arrest."

Dick and Jack took care to stand under a gas-lamp.

" Have you got two men there with a barber's pole?" asked the voice, rising from a roar to a shriek.

"Yes, sir," chuckled Bullam, gleefully, mistaking the direction of his superior's wrath. " I caught—— "

" Did n't they tell you that it was their property, bought and paid for?"

" Yes, they had some cock-and-bull—— "

" Stop!" thundered the captain, "you 're too —— ready to think every gentleman you meet is a liar. Don't you be so —— —— hot after your promotion. " If you 'll give more attention to your important duties, and less to making capital out of the students, you 'll get ahead faster. Now you go all the way back with these gentlemen, and see that they are not troubled any more. If they are brought here again I 'll know who to blame for it. I 'll have you up for a breach of special duty, and make it hot for you. What 's more, you treat them civilly. I 'll have no bullies on my squad. If this man gives you boys any lip, come around and see me about it in the morning. Now get out of here, and you, Bullam, mind what I tell you, and be —— —— careful."

All the blanks in the foregoing address were filled in with deep color, and the window went down with a slam that heavily sank in the sickened soul of the astonished Bullam.

"Come along, sergeant," cried Randolph, cheerfully, shouldering the barber-pole. He and Dick led the way back through Quincy Square, whistling the "Rogue's March" and the "Père de la Victoire." The overwhelmed Bullam fell in behind. As they turned down Harvard Street, he walked slowly and tried to drop back to a distance which would disguise his connection with the parade ; but his con-

querors allowed no such break in the procession.
They slowed down, too, and kept about ten
feet in front of him.

On the first corner of Harvard Street were
stationed three or four small boys (the occasionally useful Cambridge muckers) employed
as vedettes. Upon the approach of the triumph,
they dashed off to the different clubs and gather-
ing-places where the long oppressed people
were eagerly awaiting the arrival of Bullam
in chains. These all flocked to Harvard Street,
Hudson bringing his cornet, Dixey a pair of
cymbals, and Ned Burleigh flourishing the
drum-major's baton, with which he had done
mighty service in the last torch-light procession. It was going to be the most glorious
triumph ever seen in the classic shades since
Washington rode through them on his white
charger.

But, alas! what a trivial thing may upset the
grandest strategy; what a petty boor may
defeat Ulysses! Yet it was not such a petty
boor who caused the ruin in this case; it was
the Cambridge mucker, and he should never
have been overlooked by a man of Machiavelli
Stoughton's experience. Those who know the

Cantabrigian guerilla respect his power, though they abhor his ways. An influential member of this free lancehood, having demanded a quarter for the vedette service before mentioned, and being refused employment, nursed a vindictive spirit. He gathered a band on Harvard Street, near to the advanced scouts, and waited to see what was going to happen. As soon as Stoughton and Randolph came up with the attendant Bullam, this unforeseen enemy raised a joyful shout and marshalled his comrades behind the trio. As they proceeded along the street, he yelled to every mucker they passed, " Hey, ragsy, come on! Here 's two o' de Ha'vards gettin' run in ! "

Muckers gathered from every side like jackals, and Bullam, realizing the sudden turn in the aspect of affairs, no longer lagged behind, but forged up alongside of his would-be tamers, and assumed his old fierce and haughty air. He could maintain his dignity before the public anyway.

This was the way Dick Stoughton's great triumph looked when it reached a point opposite the Yard. The expectant crowd of undergraduates looked for a moment in surprise and grief, then, notwithstanding their disappointment at Bullam's escape, a great roar of laughter went up, as they concluded that the two daring plotters had egregiously failed in their attempt and were on their way to a dungeon.

"Let 's bail them out," cried two or three. "Bail nothing, you idiots," shouted the chagrined Stoughton, "we are not arrested ; this man is our body-guard. Come on, and we will take the procession around the Square and up Garden Street."

This had been Dick's original intention as to the line of march ; but just at this moment the Dean of Harvard College came around the corner of Holyoke Street and stopped short. In the direction of Harvard Square lay the jail, and Stoughton at once decided that a triumph of such uncertain appearance had better be brought to a close right where they were. He and Randolph halted, therefore, and, waving aloft the barber's pole, gave Bullam their gracious permission to depart. As a little extra effect they ordered him to disperse the rabble, to which mandate he payed no attention. Then, with as much dignity as possible, they retreated into Foster's. It was the best effort they could make to retrieve the day, a weak ending to so magnificent a scheme.

They did not hear the last of their "grand pageant" for a long time ; but their own recollection of it will always be softened by the memory of those sweet moments beneath the captain's window.

THE DOG BLATHERS.

BESIDES the "officers of instruction and government," and the instructed and governed, there are many classes and individuals that make up the university population of Cambridge—unofficial members, whose names do not appear in the catalogue. There are the camp followers, the goodies, the janitors, the Poco, John the Orangeman, Riley, the O'Haras who "understand th' busniz," and all the other dignitaries, as firmly established and well recognized as the Faculty. Probably the most numerous of the unofficial classes is the great four-legged one. There are undergraduate dogs, and law-school dogs, and post-graduate dogs, and I believe there were one or two Divinity dogs. During our time there were several very distinguished dogs in the Faculty, notably one huge bull-dog. Among the undergraduates, the ugliest and most perfect in form and feature, the most polished and attractive in manner, the most genial and popular, in every way the leader *par excellence*, was Rattleton's round head bull-terrier Blathers.

Blathers was named after the great man who bred him. That celebrated fancier was renowned throughout Cambridge for two things, his dogs and his profanity. He could outswear Sawin's expressman, Hitchell the black scout, and the janitor of Little's Block, and any one who could excel those three was indeed an artist. I do not believe, however, that the recording angel entered all of Blather's items in the debit column ;—in the first place, he would not have had time, in the second place, most of Blather's oaths were not delivered in anger, in the sense of Raca, but flowed out innocently and unconsciously, merely as aids to conversation. One morning this worthy came into Rattleton's room, bearing in his hand a little brindled object about five inches long. It looked like a stub-tailed rat, whose nose had been smashed with a lump of coal.

"Good mornin', Mr. Rattleton ; beg your pardon for intrudin', sir, but I 've got sumpthin' here I want for to show yer. I 've got a magnificent animal."

"Oh, get out, Blathers; I don't want a dog; had to give away the last one."

The following speech was bristling with profanity, but I have omitted even the indication blanks, except in one passage where they were too characteristic to be left out.

"I don't want yer to buy him, sir. I just want to show him to yer. He's a beauty. I know yer knows the points of a dog, sir, and its just a pleasure I'm givin' yer to look at him. Just take him in your hand, sir. Now, I sold Mrs. G. an own half brother of that feller. You know Mrs. G., surely, down here to the Theolog. school?" (Mrs. G. was a most charming and gentle lady, the wife of a celebrated clergyman.) "Well, I stopped at her house the other day to see how she liked the pup. She says to me, 'By ——, Blathers,' says she, 'that's the —— —— finest dog ever I see; d—— me, if it ain't,' says she. Yes, sir, that's just what she thought about him. You go ask her and see if it ain't. And she wouldn't say nothin' she didn't mean, just to tickle me, neither. Mrs. G. is a real lady, and knows the points of a dog, she does. She was—— ——kind to my wife when she was

6

sick last time.   Oh, my wife's been orful sick,
Mr. Rattleton.   I had to pay for a lot of doctor's consults and other stuff ; that 's just the
only reason, sir, I want to sell this beautiful
pup.   I 'd never part with him in this world, if
I could help it."

Blathers never would have parted from any
of his dogs had it not been for his frequent
family afflictions.   These afflictions were always very expensive and varied, from the
funeral of his mother to the birth of twins.
He buried four mothers in one year ; that was
his best work, though six children born during
the following term pushed hard on the record.

" If I could only make up my mind to let
yer have that dog, Mr. Rattleton," he went on,
" it would work both ways.   Maybe I ought to
do it.   It would be a favor and a kind thing in
me to sell yer that pup at any price, and you 'd
be doin' a charity to a poor man in helpin' me
along.   It would be a good action all around,
see ?   Oh, I need the money orful bad."

Rattleton during this speech had been playing with the puppy, and he was struck both by
the brightness of the little fellow and the logic
of his owner.   He knew that Blathers really did

have rather hard times with his family. In any
case Lazy Jack never took the trouble to sift a
tale of woe and apply the most enlightened and
efficient remedy. He had no excuse for not
doing so ; he took the Social Ethics Course in
Philosophy because it was easy, and of course
he knew how wrong it is to give to a beggar ;
nevertheless, he rarely failed to do so if he had
a coin in his pocket, because it was so much
easier than making enquiries and giving advice.
Moreover Jack was so lacking in principles, that
if he thought the beggar looked cold and in
want of a hot whiskey, he was, if anything,
more apt to yield the ill-destined alms. In this
instance the insidious Blathers had struck him
in two vulnerable spots, his very weak nature,
and his love of dogs. He also wanted to get
rid of Blathers with his endless stream of lurid
and decidedly rum-flavored eloquence, and the
easiest way to do so was to buy the puppy.

It was in his master's Sophomore year that
Blathers, the pup, began his career. He waxed
fast in beauty and knowledge. His nose grew
in and his teeth grew out, his ears assumed the
correct angle and his legs the proper curve.
His tail in babyhood had been scientifically

bitten off by the gentleman after whom he was named, and was, therefore, of exactly the right length. He went through the distemper and gave it to every dog in his club. His spirit did not belie his points ; before the end of his junior year he had tackled almost every dog in Cambridge and generally came out on top. He was a dog of marvellous tact, also ; he learned not to growl at the proctor on his staircase. Rattleton spent much time on Blather's education—so did Rattleton's friends. The latter, among other accomplishments, succeeded after great effort in teaching him to drink beer ; but Blathers never went beyond the bounds of propriety, as did frequently that disreputable Irish terrier of Dixey's.

Blather's most prominent virtue of all was devotion to his master, and his affection was fully returned. Those two were rarely apart, except in the mornings, before Rattleton was up. Blathers always got out with the nine o'clock lecture men and chapel goers, and would visit around at the various club-tables where he had friends, generally collecting five or six breakfasts before his master arose. At about eleven o'clock he would be seen, sitting with his arms akimbo, in front of the Holly Tree ; then Jack was sure to be inside, getting the marvellous dropped eggs from the sad-eyed John. If ever Blathers frequented the steps of Massachusetts, Sever, or other lecture hall, all men would know that Jack Rattleton was again on probation. If they saw the dog on the grim stone Stair of Sighs in the south entrance of University, they would make sympathetic inquiries when next they met the master.

When the round black and brown head stuck out of the window of Riley's cab, it was certain that Rattleton was bound over the bridge. They even went once or twice to the theatre together, Blathers concealed under Jack's overcoat. Though pugnacious by nature, it was not because Blathers loved other dogs less, but fighting more. He loved a row for its own sweet self, had few enemies and several warm friends. He was particularly devoted to Hudson's Topsy, and engaged in many a combat on her account, and for her edification. There were only two dogs for whom he had any real aversion—Mike Dixey, of his own class, and Baynor's white bull-dog, of the class below him.

Probably the happiest moment of Blathers
college life occurred one day on Holmes' Field.
There was a class ball-game going on ; the
Sophomores were ranged on one side of the
field, the Juniors opposite.   The white bull-dog
had been barking in time with the cheering,
yelping at the players of the opposing team,
trying to "rattle" the pitcher, and making
himself generally conspicuous and obnoxious.
Finally, in the excitement over some good
play, he slipped his collar and ran into the out-
field to congratulate the centre-fielder.   Somehow or other (Ned Burleigh probably knew),
Blathers happened to get loose at the same
moment.   With a heralding bark he flew into
the listed field and made straight for the white
champion.   All interest in the ball-game ceased
at once.   With a great shout the two opposing
crowds rose from the seats *en masse*, and swept
across the diamond, "blocking off" the owners
of the two dogs, who rushed to separate them.
In the rush, five or six more terriers got adrift,
and reached the front well ahead of their
masters.   In just about ten seconds there was
a ball of at least seven dogs of various fighting
breeds, rolling about in a halo of hair, howls,

and pure delight. After a few minutes, their masters succeeded in pushing through the surrounding crowd, and each man laid hold of a dog's tail or hind leg. By dint of heaving and kicking, the happy party was at last broken up, and at the bottom of the pile were found Blathers and the white bull-dog. They were locked in a fond embrace, and it took hot water from the gymnasium to get them apart. Ever after that Blathers bore a scar on the side of his head ; but he was proud of that mark, for there was a larger and more distinct one on the Sophomore dog.

Blathers got into a scrape in his Senior year that nearly caused his expulsion from the University, and compromised his master seriously. An aunt of Rattleton's came out to Cambridge one afternoon, for the purpose of attending the Thursday Vespers in Appleton Chapel. She notified Jack that she expected him to escort her. Jack got his room in order, with some difficulty, expurgated the ornaments and pictures, put his aunt's photograph on the mantel-piece and a Greek lexicon on the table, and sent Blathers to spend the afternoon with a friend. Aunt could not abide a dog, especially one of Blathers' type of beauty. So Mr. B. went off with Jack Randolph.

Randolph's room was in the back of Thayer, and his window commanded the approaches to Appleton Chapel. Blathers was squatted in the window-seat with his head on one side, idly watching the birds, and wondering where his master could have gone. Suddenly his eye fell on that very person, and with him one of that kind of humans whose legs are all in one piece. Blathers had seen lots of that kind, and knew well enough what they were; but what could one of them possibly be doing with his master, right here in Cambridge, at this time of year? He had never seen such a thing as that before, except once on Class Day. It was for this, then, that he had been dismissed for the afternoon! Well, well, well, pretty goings on! He betrayed his astonishment and irritation by a low " wuff ! " jumped down from the window-seat, and scratched at the door.

" No," said Randolph, looking at him, " you can't get out. Did you see a cat ? "

Blathers came over to the armchair, stood up, putting both hands on Randolph's knees, and looked at him appealingly.

"Yes, I know," said Randolph, "your master has deserted you for the afternoon, has n't he? Mean trick, is n't it? And where do you suppose he has gone? To Vespers, think of that! Don't shake your head, Blathers, it 's true—— " " Wuff ! " " Yes, rather re-markable, I know; no wonder you say so. But don't blame him ; he could n't help it, and it will do him good."

A few minutes afterwards Randolph threw away his book, and took his cap.

"Come, Blathers," said he, "we 'll go over to the Pud for awhile. You may find your friend Topsy there."

No sooner had he opened the door than Blathers scrambled down-stairs with that grace-ful motion peculiar to a terrier on urgent busi-ness ; his hind-quarters shoved his head all the way downstairs, and tripped over it at the bot-tom. He shot out of the door as if after a cat, whisked round the corner, and made straight for the Chapel. On the steps, however, he paused, for, at that moment, coming up the path from Memorial, he saw a sight that made his blood boil. Hudson and Dixey were strolling back from the Agassiz, and trotting

ahead of them were Topsy and that abominable Mike Dixey. As has been mentioned
before, Mike was a dog of very loose character.
He would get intoxicated on beer whenever he
could find any one to " set it up." He belonged
nominally to Dixey, but was really a sort of
dog-about-college. He would attach himself
to any one whom he could work for crackers
and beer. He did not mind spending the
night on a door-step, and associated with all
the street curs. He would hang around the
public billiard-rooms and Foster's, and do tricks
for sandwiches. Sometimes he would disappear
on a spree for days, get caught by the muckers,
and come home with a tin can in tow. Altogether he was no fit company for a lady, and
when Blathers saw this low-lived animal walking with his Topsy, reverence for the spot
could not restrain his indignation. Right in
front of the Chapel door he insulted the Irish
terrier, and before the men behind could come
up, then and there the fight began. Rattleton,
within, heard the sounds of conflict rise above
the anthem, and, by some vague intuition, his
blood ran cold. Another moment and Mike
came flying up the aisle with yelps of pain,

evidently seeking sanctuary. Blathers may have had a deep reverence for Appleton Chapel (barring the architecture), but his blood was up, and he did not stop to think. He pursued the flying foe, overtook and grabbed him again, just beyond Rattleton's pew, and alongside of that of a couple of magnates. Jack thought it would be better to remove those two dogs himself, and did so, one in each hand. But there was no use in pretending that he did not know to whom that scientific bull-terrier belonged. The men outside had some difficulty in persuading him that they were in no way responsible for the episode.

Mr. Blathers lived long and went to many places, but that was the only time he ever attended services in church.

THAT evening at dinner Burleigh and Rattleton entertained the table with a glowing description of a new play they had seen on the previous night, at the Howard Athenæum. They were most enthusiastic about it.

" I can't understand," declared Burleigh, " how such a piece and such a troupe happened to drop into the old Howard. Such scenery! Why, the stage setting was the best I ever saw. One act was laid in the pine woods ; you could look way through them, apparently, live birds flew about among the branches, and they must have burned some sort of balsam in the wings, for you could actually smell the pines."

" That 's a new smell for the Howard," remarked Hudson.

" Yes, and those two girls!" added Jack Rattleton. " By Jove, was n't that blonde a beauty ! "

" The brunette was better," averred Burleigh. " How she did sing ! They have splendid songs all through the play."

" Never saw such acting," said Jack, " even —certainly never at the Howard."

" The hero was a magnificent young man," Burleigh went on. " You ought to see him throw down the villain in the last act. I 'm going again as soon as I can."

" Why have n't we heard of it before ? " queried Stoughton, suspiciously.

" It was a first night," explained Burleigh, promptly. " Jack and I were pioneers. You fellows ought to go see it. You 'll hear enough of it before it is over ; but go in now while it is fresh."

" I have nothing to do to-night," said Hudson. " I believe I 'll go. Who is with me ? "

Stoughton and Gray both agreed to join him. Holworthy and Randolph were going to drive over to a ball in Brookline.

" I 'd give anything· to go with you chaps," said Burleigh, " but I have got to work into the wee sma' hours on my forensic. It is due to-morrow morning, and I have n't done a thing on it."

" I 'd like to see that show again, too," said

Jack, "but I don't feel very well to-night. I 'm going to turn in early."

The three theatre-goers started for town immediately after dinner. They stopped at one of the clubs first, and picked up three or four other men on the strength of Burleigh's eulogy of the play.

Whoever has been through Harvard College and never been to the Howard Athenæum has neglected his advantages; fortunately such deplorable instances are rare. Who, that has improved his opportunities, does not remember the old stamping-ground, where the commingled perfumes of orange-peel, humanity, and pea-nuts would smell to high heaven, were they not stopped in a concentrated mass by the grimy roof. There things are real, things are earnest, unweakened by affectation and refinement. The villains are real bad villians, and carry knives, not cigarettes. They know how to gloat. The heroes have red undershirts and true nobility, and don't mind showing either. The heroines are not ashamed of sentimentality. Neither is the audience. There, too, is music that you can remember and whistle, that you can sing afterwards on the way back to Cambridge ; not music that you must contemplate with rapt gaze on the ceiling. There you will find humor of the broad, plain, unmistakable variety, humor at which you can laugh for its own sake, not for the maker's wit or your own in detecting it. Nor, in that shrine of the Muses, does pleasure always end with the fall of the curtain. Frequently you may see two or three excellent fights on the way out, and perhaps be granted a share in one yourself. Oh, you get your money's worth at the classic Athenæum, for it is all for fifty cents (thirty-five in the gallery).

" I have a suspicion," said Stoughton, on the way in town, " that those fellows were lying to us. I 'll bet this show is something awful, they were probably bored to death, and conceived the happy thought of getting us sold in the same way."

" Never mind," said Hudson, philosophically ; "we 'll have a good time anyway."

Before the curtain had been up ten minutes, Dick's suspicion gained ground ; it's truth was fully confirmed long before the end of the play. The scenery, the birds, and the pine balsam effects were wholly creatures of Burleigh's capable brain; as for Jack Rattleton's houris, Stoughton declared that "Noah was a fool to have saved them; he ought to have shut them out in the rain long enough to get a wash any way."

Even the Athenæum audience was dissatisfied and inclined to jeer. Gray wanted to leave at the end of the first act.

"Hold on," insisted Hudson, "let's stay here and make this a success. There's lots of good sentiment all through it, just your style Gray. All it needs is a little enthusiasm in the house to warm up the actors. Let's lead the applause on the strong points."

So they stayed, and their efforts were attended with such success, that they might have had a free pass for future performances. Every time the hero said, "I am the just man and you are the villain," or the heroine declared she would never leave him while life lasted, or showed other symptoms of heroism, the knot of students would stamp, and applaud, and rouse the finer feelings of the whole house. The grateful actors certainly did warm up, and delivered with more and more vim their honest expressions of lofty sentiment and occasional touches of patriotism, the latter utterly uncalled for, but always welcome. The audience became worked up as well, but in the last act suddenly began to hiss.

"Hullo! what's up now?" asked Gray, who had not taken the Athenæum course faithfully, and was not learned in it; "what are they hissing at?"

"Good gracious, man," answered Hudson, "don't you see? Don't display your ignorance. They are hissing the villain. It's the greatest compliment you can pay him. Go ahead, hiss like a good one."

On the whole, the performance was a grand success, and Hudson insisted that Gray had made an undoubted conquest of the second lady. After it was over some one mentioned "broiled lob. and musty," at Parks, but it was voted to return to Cambridge and make a rare-bit there.

"We'll go pull out Ned Burleigh, and have it in his room," suggested Dick.

"No you don't!" exclaimed Hudson. "You forget I'm his chum. I'll have no Welsh rare-bit made in that room unless we draw lots and I get stuck. The room would smell of cheese and stale beer for twenty-four hours."

7

" Let 's land on Rattleton then. We 'll teach him to lie."

Feeling in a luxurious mood they scorned the cars, and chartered a herdic, four men getting inside and three on the roof. For those readers who know not the herdic, I will explain that it is a sort of tiny omnibus in which four thin people can sit uncomfortably. It usually has two wheels and never more than one horse —sometimes not quite as much.

" I may as well tell you before we start," said Stoughton, who sat on the top, to the driver, " that we are not Freshmen, so don't break a spring on the bridge and tell us that it will cost you ten dollars to get it mended."

" I know you 're old hands," answered Jehu, with a grin, " I know youse fellers. I remember your face pertickler. Mebbe you disrecollect comin' out with me one night from Parker's. Let 's see, guess it was two years ago, after the Institoot dinner."

" All right, my friend, say no more," acknowledged Dick, as the other two men shouted. " The drink is on me. Here is the price of it."

The door at the back of the herdic is held

shut with a strap that leads through the roof
to the driver's seat. This was secured firmly,
so as to keep the inside passengers safe, for it
is an established courtesy for those inside to
slip out when near the college, leaving the
others to pay the driver and joining them later.
By means of the strap, however, and the lack
of a knife among the insiders, all arrived well
together at the building where Rattleton
roomed.

"I'll go to the Fly and get the cheese and
beer," said Gray. "You get your chafing-dish,
Dick."

Stoughton roomed in the same building with
Rattleton, as did Hudson and Burleigh. While
he went after his chafing-dish the others recon-
noitered Rattleton's quarters. The door was
locked and all was dark. The glass ventilator
over the door, however, was unfastened, and
large enough to admit a man. Jack Rattleton
always left his ventilator unfastened, for he
often depended on it for his own ingress. The
reason of this was very simple,—the door had a
spring bolt, and it was characteristic of Mr.
Rattleton's nature to frequently leave his keys
inside and shut the door when he went out.

It was a very simple matter for Hudson to climb over the door through this ventilator, drop down, and open the door from the inside.

"Look out for Blathers," said one man. "If that pretty pup is in there he'll take a piece out of your leg."

"He knows my voice," answered Hudson, as he "shinned" over. He let the rest in and lit the gas. Rattleton was not in his bedroom.

"Humph," grunted Hudson. "Said he was n't well and was going to turn in early. The abominable liar."

They poked up the fire and had it roaring when Stoughton returned, bearing the chafing-dish and a long pipe, his dear Mary Jane.

"That's a good idea," said Hudson, as his eye fell on the latter article. "You've brought that disgusting black pipe. We can stand it for a while, and it will permeate Jack's room and teach him the beauty of truth. Puff away on Mary; serve Jack right."

Rattleton's plates and other necessities were foraged out by the time Gray appeared with the cheese and beer. Not seeing Rattleton, he asked how the others had got in. Hudson explained. "This open ventilator habit of

Jack's " he added, " is worse than rooming on the ground floor. Ned Burleigh and I had enough of that in Freshman year, before we moved up here. Our room was a regular darned club. Everybody would drop in there between lectures, chin when we wanted to study, and smoke our tobacco, just because it was too much trouble to go up-stairs. We could n't leave our window open at night without having some fools crawl in, at any time after midnight, and raise the deuce."

" Yes, I remember. It was very pleasant," remarked Stoughton.

The creation of the rarebit was well under way with the usual accompaniment of advice and altercation over the ingredients, when shouts were heard from under the window, of " Jack, Jack Rat, Oh, Jack ! "

Hudson threw up the window and saw Holworthy and Randolph below in a buggy. " Mr. Rattleton is not in, gentlemen," he said, " but come right up and make yourselves at home."

" All right ; be with you in a moment, as soon as we have taken this trap round to Blake's."

" It is the two society fritterlings," announced Hudson, as he drew in his head. A few minutes later Randolph and Holworthy appeared in their big coats.

"Seems to me you 're back from your ball pretty early," observed Gray.

"Hol did n't find the person there he wanted to see, so he soured on the whole thing and dragged me away early," Jack Randolph explained.

"What a whopper," said Holworthy, as he took off his ulster. "It was very stupid, and Jack himself suggested that we should be happier in Cambridge."

"Aha," cried Stoughton, who was stirring the "bunny" with a master hand. "Very nice. Two gentlemen in faultless evening attire. They 'll do for the waiters. Here, quick, hand up your plates before this thing gets cold."

While they were eating the rarebit, a step was heard in the entry, accompanied by the trotting feet of a dog, and the locked door was tried. Then a familiar voice drawled "What the devil is going on in here?"

"Hullo, Jack," cried Stoughton, "come right in. Don't be bashful."

"Open the door, you arrant burglars," demanded Rattleton. " My keys are on my bureau, or somewhere inside. "

" Climb over the transom as I did," Hudson called. " You 'll have to turn your back to the company in the performance, but don't mind the awkwardness of the position."

" We 'll excuse your back. We have your hair-brushes and the fire shovel already," added Randolph, cheerily.

" Don't be such babies," said Jack, (whenever any of the gang was at a disadvantage, he was apt to age suddenly) " come, let me in."

" Are you sorry you told a naughty fib to-night ?" asked Hudson, with his hand on the knob.

" Yes."

" Will you set up the ingredients for a punch ?"

" Yes."

" All right then, you may come in," said Hudson, graciously, opening the door.

" How was the play ?" inquired Jack, pleasantly, as he went into his bedroom after the wash-basin, the regular understudy for a punch-bowl.

" Enjoyed it immensely, in spite of your wishes for our entertainment," Hudson declared. " We know now your ideal of talent and beauty."

" Don't blame me. That was all Burleigh's rot," protested Jack, apologetically, but with a chuckle. " Why don't you pull him out ? "

" That is a good plan," assented Hudson. " Two of you come up and help me capture the elephant. He may resist." A committee of three went up to wait upon Burleigh.

" What is the sense of this meeting as to the temperature of the grog ? " asked Rattleton.

" Hot ! " promptly moved the two who had driven over from Brookline. The motion was carried, so Jack put the kettle on the fire.

" Speaking of the drama and brother Burleigh," said Holworthy, " do you remember the time, Dick, that we saw the old man suping in that spectacular play in Sophomore year ? "

" I 'm not likely to forget it," answered Dick. " You fellows remember that show called ' Albrachia,' or some such name, full of red fire and fairies ? Hol. and I went in to see it one night, and whom should we discover as leading demon in the grand climax, but the stout

Edward. We nearly stood up and cheered,—
but we 'll make him tell about it to-night."

" Hullo, here is the sylph now ! " exclaimed
some one, as the committee returned in triumph
with Ned in tow.

" The perjured loafer told us he was going to
work on his forensic," cried Hudson. " Look
at this," pointing to Burleigh, whose generous
proportions were swathed in gaudy pajamas.

" I hear you enjoyed the play exceedingly,"
remarked Burleigh, as he made for the fireplace,
and spread his huge form all over the front
of it.

" So we did, no thanks to you," answered
Gray.

" Any men who are such Athenæum Lotha-
rios as to be decoyed in town by the mere
mention of two pretty actresses, deserve to get
sold," declared Ned, severely.

" Here, take your toddy and stop your
mouth," said Stoughton. " As a penance for
your lies, you can give us some reminiscences
of your disreputable career on the stage."

After some demurring, Burleigh was persuaded to begin his yarn. The " tea " was
made by this time, and enthroned on the stu-

dent's desk in the centre of the room. With "tod and tobac." the party disposed itself about the room, every one with a view more to ease than grace. Blathers, as usual, chose his master's outstretched legs. Ned Burleigh, with a cigar, stood in front of the fire in his airy raiment, his feet apart, warming his exterior with the genial blaze, and his interior with the genial toddy. Would that we could have those evenings again !

THE HARVARD LEGION AT PHILIPPI.

"WHAT do you want me to relate?" asked Burleigh. "The great battle of Philippi?"

"Yes, we would like to hear about that," answered Stoughton, "and also your experience with the Hosts of Darkness."

"That was a very short and painful affair," Ned explained. "I 'll tell you that first. You must know, my children, that I was once a godless Sophomore even as other Sophs. You may scarcely believe it now, but I was. Among other follies, I took to 'suping' occasionally. Of course my intentions were purely noble; I wanted to elevate the stage. On one occasion this man Hudson, here, led me to the Boston Theatre, where an elaborate show was being given and 'supes' were in demand. You fellows must remember the play, it was called 'Alboraka, the Wizard.' They wanted only one man for that night, and as I was the hand-

somer, they chose me.   I comforted Steve by
promising to share with him the quarter that I
expected to earn ; I believe on the strength of
my promise he bought a seat in the peanut
gallery."

"Oh, no, I did n't," interrupted Hudson, " I
had a seat right under a box where there was a
theatre-party of Mrs. Mayflor Tremont's, with
a lot of girls I knew.   I was thundering glad I
was n't on the stage, and had more than half a
mind to point you out to them."

"You would n't have troubled me at all,"
answered Ned.   " That is where we unknown
woolly Westerners get the drop on the Boston
men, and you dudes who go in for Boston
society.   However, to go on with this confession, I was appointed leader of the Hosts of
Darkness.   I don't know why I was singled
out for this distinction, unless it was on account
of my superb figure."

"That was it," corroborated Stoughton.
"You did look stunning in those red tights,
even more fetching than you are now in those
pajamas."

"The part was not a difficult one, but very
important," Burleigh continued.   "I had to

look fierce, and bear aloft a huge red and gold
affair. This was referred to once or twice as
' yon gonfalon of Diabolus,' so I suppose that 's
what it was. I only had to go on the stage
twice. In the last scene, where the Wizard
got thrown down, there was a high bridge at
the back of the stage. It was steep on the
sides, shaped a good deal like the Chinese
bridge in a blue willow-ware plate; don't you
remember? I had to hold this bridge for the
Wizard at the head of my minions, and was
doing it with dignity and grace. My instructions were to stay there until the Queen of the
Fairies should point at me and say 'Avaunt,
vile blood-fiends, to the shades below'; then
to retire with signs of rage and terror, while
the Hosts of Light came up the other side of
the bridge. Now I was watching and listening
to the Queen carefully, and I am sure she never
pointed at me, or opened her head about
' avaunting.' I think myself that my fatal
beauty in the red tights had made an impression on her, and she did n't want me to leave.
She probably could n't find it in her heart to
call me a blood-fiend; at any rate there was
some hitch, for the Hosts of Light began

coming up the bridge ahead of time. Of course, I was n't going to avaunt without orders, so I stood there waiting for my cue. The leading angel called me a most vile name, in an anxious undertone, and poked his spear violently in the pit of my stomach. He hurt me like the devil, so I promptly smashed him on the head with the Gonfalon of Diabolus, and bowled him down among the advancing Hosts of Light, to their utter confusion. The next minute something lit on the back of my neck, and that is all I know. I believe it was a sandbag hove from the wings, and that I was dragged out by the heels."

"You were, you were," Holworthy shouted at the recollection, "but it was done so quickly that half of the audience did n't see it."

"When I came to," Ned went on, "I was on my face behind the scenes, with four or five able-bodied Irishmen sitting on my back. The 'super' captain was going to turn me over to the cop; but I begged pardon all round, paid for the leading angel's broken head, and finally managed to smooth things over."

"They are pretty careful how they take amateur supes at any of the theatres now.

Nothing like the battle of Philippi can ever occur again," said Rattleton, regretfully.

"Give us that, Ned," said Stoughton ; "I guess some of these fellows have never heard an accurate account by one of the heroes."

"That was truly the grandest suping event in history," said Burleigh, refilling his glass, and returning to his position by the fire. "It was just after that new theatre was opened, way down there on Washington Street. It was a cheap shrine, but I tell you, now, Melpomene was right in it. The owners had no idea of making it a low-down variety hall, not much. They were going to give high-class perform-ances and educate the masses. One of the first things they had there was a Shakespearean re-vival, run by a peripatetic star named Riley. The fellows used to go in and supe all the time. They rather liked to have Harvard men for two reasons: first, because it was cheap, and, in the second place, I think Riley's manager rather expected us to bring all our friends and rela-tives there to see us act, and give the place a boom.

"The first night of *Julius Cæsar* came on Jim de Laye's twenty-first birthday, and he

was going to give a dinner, after which we intended to fill a box at the show and give
Cæsar a good send-off. I went in town to get
the box, and at the office I heard the manager,
or some official, complaining about lack of
supes. I made inquiries, and it ended in my
contracting to furnish him with ten good men
and true for that evening at reasonable rates.
He gave me as a bonus a few tickets for any
of my family or 'lady friends.' It showed how
green he was to take ten of 'de Ha'vards' at
once. They never would have done that anywhere else in town.

" The other chaps all fell in with the arrangement, and we had the dinner at Parker's early.
A man does not get to be twenty-one years old
every day in the year, so we took pains to see
that Jim did it properly.

" That lazy goat on the sofa there (pointing
to Rattleton) had not been seen in Cambridge
that afternoon, and knew nothing about the
suping arrangement. Of course, he was late to
dinner, as usual, and of course, as usual, he
turned up with that d——d dog of his. After
dinner, when we adjourned to the theatre, we
wanted him to leave Blathers behind at Par-

ker's, but he insisted on taking the pup along, wrapped in his overcoat. He assured us that Blathers would keep perfectly quiet, and no one would ever know he was there. We might have known better, but I suppose we were in a yielding mood. De Laye and two or three others brought bottles of fizz in their overcoats. They said it was always well to propitiate the natives, and thought such provisions might be popular with the Thespians. Jim swore he 'd make noble Romans of every man of 'em. We got there early, and Blathers was tied up and hidden away under Jack's coat in a corner of the dressing-room. In the performance we all did our parts like little men. Rome was proud of her citizens that day. As for our mob-work, that showed positive genius."

" How Marc Antony's speech over the body did go ! " chuckled Rattleton from the sofa.

" The stage-manager was delighted and complimented us, and so did Riley himself. Jack Rat had made friends with Riley very early in the game. He had invited him out to lunch in Cambridge, and had hinted at getting him to coach the Pudding show. Moreover, Jack and I had steered several large parties in to Riley's

8

performances, and Riley knew it. It was a lucky thing for us, as it turned out, that he and Jack had got so chummy.

"All went well until the battle scene. They had put us all on the same side; in fact, we constituted the entire army of Brutus—that was another evidence of greenness in the management. The battle had been raging mildly for some time. We had marched and counter-marched, and had been reviewed and exhorted two or three times, without even getting a glimpse of the enemy. At last it came to the scene where Brutus' aggregation gets driven across the stage by Antony's offering a desperate resistance. Cassius had been killed, young Cato was going to be captured, and everything was going to the bow-wows. While we were standing in the wings along with Antony's army, waiting to go on, Jim de Laye said, ' Hang it, let 's put a little real good acting into this thing; these stage scraps are too woodeny.' Of course I did my best to restrain this idea among my companions, but it became popular at once in spite of anything I could say. I must confess I always had rather a desire myself to see that oily-mouthed peep of a

Marc Antony well thrashed. The next minute we had to go across the back of the stage,
hotly contesting every inch of the way with
our trusty wooden brands, two up and two
down. About half way over, that crazy Jim
de Laye opened the ball by smiting his man
hip and thigh and other parts, in the most life-
like manner. The other supe hit back in just
anger, and there was an instant rally of the
Brutus forces. My man was a little fellow, and
I did him up in time to see an entirely new
feature introduced in the scene. Marc Antony
himself suddenly appeared, hard pressed by a
togaed citizen. The way he got there was this
—correct me, Jack, if I make any mistake in
this part of the history. Blathers, as I told
you, had been left curled up under a coat in
the dressing-room. Some of the employees
had found him there, however, untied him, and
started in to play with him. Mr. Blathers, finding himself in strange company, slipped away
from them and went looking for his master.
Just as the battle scene began, he arrived at
the wings, where Marc Antony was waiting to
go on. Antonius was in very bad humor about
something. He asked in fluent Latin, 'What

the —— that dog was doing there?' and made a kick at Blathers. I guess Blathers was in much the same mood, for he turned around and effected a prompt connection with the calf of Marc Antony's leg. He was a disappointed dog; he got his mouth full of horsehair. Antony was n't touched, and let Blathers have it with the other foot.

"Now, Jack had not been assigned to the army, and was off duty in that scene. He was standing in the wings in Roman citizen's clothes, trying to flirt with the vestal virgins.

"Hold on," interrupted Jack, "you told me to correct any mistake. That's one."

"Well, perhaps they were not. You know more about that than I do," admitted Ned. "Any way, he turned around just in time to see his faithful hound doing somersaults from Marc Antony's toe. I'll do Jack the justice to say that he is generally slow to wrath—he is too lazy—but when that ugly pup of his is concerned, he loses his head.

"He not only lost his head that time, but tried to knock off Marc Antony's too. Marc went staggering out into the field of battle, and Jack, the fool, followed him up. As I said, the battle had opened in earnest all along the line when this happened, and the house was already on it 's feet. It was a good, warm house. It was mainly from Sou' Boston, and had taken about thirty-five seconds to get on to the magnificent realism of the scene. It went wild with delight at this addition to the affair. Blathers rallied and flew out on the stage to the support of Jack's charge. This time he tore all the padding off Marc's legs, amid the enthusiastic plaudits of the audience.

"The stage-manager yelled for the policeman, and went tearing about after him. 'Colonel' Dixey, of Kentucky, who was also off duty in this scene, had enticed the cop into a distant corner, along with the departed Cæsar and a bottle of fizz. J. Cæsar was a tragedian who would have been dear to the heart of a *Puck* artist. He was a thirsty soul with a radiant nose and a beery eye. Shortly after his death he had attached himself to Colonel Dixey and his overcoat, and the Colonel had warmly requited his affection. In fact, Dixey devoted two whole bottles to the good work, and at the end of the fourth act Cæsar had had some difficulty in doing his own ghost. He was free after that, and during this last act, he and the Colonel had let in the blue-coat, and retired into a secluded nook among the scenery. The Colonel had filled Cæsar up to the brim, and had got the law pretty well zigged, too, when the manager brought the news of battle. All three rushed to the front, the cop, of course, getting there last. The conflict was at its height, when dead Cæsar appeared, boiling drunk, and took sides with inspiring shouts against his own avengers. Dixey pitched in too, and these reinforcements turned the tide at once. Brutus was victorious at all points. We rushed Marc Antony and his gang clear off the field, and destroyed the flying remnants behind the wings. The audience fairly howled and encored wildly.

" The cop was utterly useless, he grabbed the small man that I had floored in the beginning of the row, clubbed him a little, and hung on to him like grim death. The manager was crazy, and told him to send for a hurry-up wagon, and run us all in. We showed the law great respect, though, after the shindy was over; called him sergeant and offered to support him in maintaining the peace. He did n't

know exactly who was responsible, so he contented himself with shaking the little man some
more, and declaring that he could 'attend to
this business alone, and did n't want no help,
see ?' Marc Antony wanted the blood of Jack
and Blathers, but Riley, the star, who played
Brutus, was inclined to think that Antony
was to blame for the whole thing. You see
Antony had got more applause than Brutus
all through. His great speech had had a particular success, probably due to our able pre-
sentation of the populace. Riley sat on Marc
first, and then they both went for Cæsar, who
was maudlin in the corner. He had got a
helmet on, wrong side before, and was begging
us with tears in his eyes to go " once more into
the breach, dear friends, or close the wall with
our English dead." When Brutus cursed him he
drew himself up and hiccoughed, ' Et tu, Brute,
—hic—well—hic you seen me at Philippi
anyhow.'

" Riley went back on the stage and made a
little speech, and the audience cheered him to
the echo. Then the play went on, Brutus
died like a man, and all the principals, including J. Cæsar and Blathers, were called before

the curtain. Jack made it up with Marc Antony, and after the show we consoled the vanquished army with what was left of the champagne. Most of the supes were Irish, anyway, and had enjoyed the pleasantry."

IN THE EARLY SIXTIES.

IT was ten o'clock and time for John Stuart
Mill to give place to Mary Jane, so Stoughton
threw the former into an arm-chair and took
the latter from the mantel-piece. He filled
and lighted her affectionately, and the content
of the evening pipe came upon him. Then he
bethought him of beer and pleasant converse,
and strolled around to the Pudding in pursuit
thereof.

There he found the usual ten o'clock "resting convention" in session beneath its blue
cloud of nicotine. The "earnest resters," as
Burleigh termed them, were stretched about in
various attitudes, more of laziness than repose.
They were just then engaged in the popular
pastime of blackguarding the last number of
the *Lampoon* for the benefit of Hudson, one of
the editors.

"Hullo, Dick," remarked that gentleman,
glad to change the subject as Stoughton en-

tered, " we knew you were coming ; smelt Mary
Jane as soon as you turned the corner."

" Did you, really," replied Stoughton, making
room for himself on the sofa by removing
Rattleton's legs to a neighboring chair, and
spilling the dog Blathers on the floor. " What
was that chum of yours doing in the building
last night? Were you also engaged in the
unseemly disturbance?"

" No," answered Hudson, " I had nothing to
do with it. I decline all responsibility for
Edward Burleigh. I am not my room-mate's
keeper."

" I heard him carolling on the stairs at an
hour when singing should be left to the little
birds. He hammered on my door for a while,
but I knew enough not to get up. I wonder
he did n't raise the proctor. He shouted,
through my key-hole, something about the war
being over."

" Yes," said Hudson, " that was what he told
me when he woke me up by sitting on my
chest. He was going to carry the good news
all through the Yard, but I persuaded him to
go to bed and wait until morning."

" Where had he been ?"

"Well, you see, Jack Randolph carried him off yesterday evening to a meeting of the Southern Club, as an invited guest, to span the bloody chasm with him. They spanned it a good many times there, I guess, and then as it was a beautiful moonlight night and perfect sleighing, they decided that the bloody chasm ought to be spanned in Brookline and other neighboring towns. So they got a cutter, and must have conducted spanning operations on a wide scale all over the country, for they did n't get back until dawn. George Smith, the police-man, says he saw them sitting on the steps of Harvard Hall, singing 'John Brown's Body' and 'Dixie,' and hymns of peace while the sun rose."

"I deny the aspersion on the Southern Club," exclaimed 'Colonel' Dixey, from the other end of the long sofa. "I was present at the meet-ing, and we had nothing to induce sunrise hymns. I don't know what Jack and Ned did afterwards, but they did n't get it at the Southern Club."

This somewhat veiled assertion raised an in-credulous chorus: "Oh, Dixey, may you be forgiven." "Come, come, Colonel, do you

mean to persuade us that an organization con-
taining at least three members from Kentucky
is run on a cold-water basis?" "Where is the
glory of your old commonwealth?" "Bet the
meeting was full of rum—rum and rebellion!
Don't deny it, Colonel." "Drink and treason!"

"Neither, sir, neither," replied Dixey to this
chaff. "I grieve to hear such narrow-minded ac-
cusations. Prexy was there and made a speech.
—Oh, Holworthy! You know that man we
saw yesterday in the Transept of Memorial?
He was at the Southern Club with Prexy."

"Oh, yes," said Holworthy, "who was he?"

"A grad. from Georgia. I have forgotten his
name."

"I thought he was a grad., and not a stranger,
for he did n't have a guide book, and did n't
ask us to show him the "*campus*." Had he
been a soldier?"

"Did n't say. If so, he was probably a Confed."

"Well, he looked like an interesting old cock
anyway," said Holworthy to the others. "He
was standing before one of the tablets with his
hat off. Somehow, when we saw him, our own
hats felt so uncomfortable that we took them
off, too, as we passed through."

" Holly made up all sorts of poetry about him," added Dixey.

" No, I did n't ; but I do think he did the right thing in uncovering."

"Of course he did," said Ernest Gray, emphatically. "No man ought to keep his hat on in that transept."

"Oh, now you 've done it, Hol," groaned Stoughton. "You have started the 'Only Serious.'"

" We get too careless going back and forth in it every day," continued Gray. "We don't fully appreciate it, or we forget what it means."

" Forget what it means ! Great Scott, Ernest, have you never heard a Class Day oration or poem ? What would our inspired youths do without the poor, hard-worked old transept ? How did they ever get inspired before it was built ? Don't we have our hearts fired all up at least once a year on that subject ?"

"Except those of us who may have been previously fired by the Dean," put in Rattleton, with a contemplative sigh over eminent possibilities.

"Well, it is a pity then that the Class Day conflagration does n't last a little longer. I don't believe in keeping sentiment for special occasions. It would be better for all hands to preserve a little of it throughout the year, and in this place, of all others, I should think at least a little reverence for the past might be kept alive. But one might suppose that there was no such thing as reverence at Harvard nowadays."

"Hooray!" "Hear, hear!" "Go it, old man!" "Good for the Only Serious!" "Pegasus in a canter!"

"That's right," answered Gray warmly, to this burst of invidious encouragement. "Laugh at anything that is serious or the least approach to feeling; it is the fashion."

"Brought on by over-doses of gush," remarked Stoughton, knocking the ashes contemptuously out of Mary Jane.

"Of course, there is a lot of twaddle talked about such things," answered Gray, "and I acknowledge that exaggeration tends to cheapen patriotism, but the existence of a lot of tinsel in the world doesn't make gold less valuable, does it?"

"Quite true," assented Hudson, "and because Dick Stoughton smokes such a pipe as

Mary Jane, there is no reason why we should all give up tobacco. That is a better simile than yours."

"Well, it is a good thing that Harvard men have not always been so afraid of appearing in earnest," growled Gray. "I don't believe there was so much brilliant wit wasted when men were leaving college every day to join their regiments. I wish I had been here then." .

"So do I," drawled Rattleton; "what a bully excuse a fellow would have had for not getting his degree."

"What an excitement there must have been," went on Gray, without noticing the interruption. "Just think of being cheered out of the Yard when you left for the war, and then perhaps distinguishing yourself, and coming back to Class Day with your arm in a sling."

"Just think of coming back in a pine-box," added Hudson, graphically.

"Well, suppose you did? You have got to die some time, and your name would have been put on a tablet in memorial."

"Yes, but you would n't have been tickled by seeing it there," said the irritating Stoughton. " Half your patriotism is vanity, Ernest, you shallow theatrical poser."

" It would do you men good to read the *Memorial Biographies*," Gray continued, now thoroughly aroused, and paying no attention to the side remarks. " They ought to be part of the prescribed work for a degree."

" Yes, but as Hudson says, you could n't do that if you were a biographee," reasoned Dane Austin, the law-school man, taking a hand in the baiting.

" It would be perfectly disgusting to hear you fellows talk this way," Gray declared, " if one did n't know that it was all affectation. I am not sure that that fact does not make it worse. You all really feel just as I do, but you are afraid to say so."

" Another appalling case of Harvard indifference," observed Stoughton. " The modern dilettante has no noble desire for red war."

" He likes to make people believe that he has no noble desire for anything, and he has a morbid fear of being a hypocrite. As a matter of fact, you are all of you the worst kind of hypocrites, for you try to appear worse than you are."

"Oh, dear, no," Rattleton protested, lazily, "that would be too hard work for any of this crowd—except me."

"A war would be a good thing to stir you up. I almost wish the war times would come again," exclaimed Gray, hotly.

"Now you are getting right down to work," laughed Hudson. "What a rise we are getting out of our earnest young man to-night."

"You let your feelings get away with you, Gray," added Holworthy. "I don't believe it was all glory and enthusiasm in those days. You forget there was another side to it. For instance, Jack Randolph's governor was not cheered out of the Yard when *he* left for the war."

"Yes, there *was* another side to it," came a voice from the other end of the room, and a big arm-chair, that had been facing the fire with its back to the knot of men, was pushed around so as show its occupant. He was evidently one of that wide class known to the un-undergraduate as the "Old Grads." An old grad. attains his title as soon as he ceases to be a very young grad.; there is no transition degree. In this case he seemed about middle

9

aged, perhaps fifty, with hair turning gray, and
a rather deeply marked brown face.   The latter
was just then a little flushed, and had the expression often seen on a face that has just been
looking a long time into a fire and a long way
through it.

The lounging students started a little at this
sudden interruption, and stirred as young men
do on finding themselves suddenly in the presence of an older one.   Rattleton took his long
legs down from their supporting chair, Hudson
pushed his hat back from his nose to its proper
place, Dixey took his hands out of his pockets
and sat up straight, while Dick Stoughton
paused in the act of relighting Mary Jane, and
when the match burnt his fingers forbore to
swear.   As the cause of the disturbance rose
and came towards them they stood up.   Hollis
Holworthy showed signs of positive uneasiness.
He turned bright red in the face, as he recognized the man whom he had just described as
" an interesting old cock."

"I—I beg your pardon, sir," he began, " I
had no idea—— "

" That the old cock was present ? " laughed
the older man.   " I assure you, my boy, that I

was not in the least offended, and even had I
cause for offence, I deserved it. Your remark
was a retribution, a striking repetition of history. I remember once asking Holworthy of
'61 who the bully old boy in the beaver hat
was, and the bully old boy proved to be Holworthy '32. Thirty years are like a spy-glass—
your views depend upon the end through which
you look."

The thirty years melted at once beneath the
laugh that followed this introduction, and, as
the stranger took a chair among the group, the
smoke went up again from Mary Jane and
other pipes.

" Then you were in college with my father?"
asked Holworthy. "You must have been here
just in the time of which we were speaking."

" That is the reason why I took the liberty
of joining so abruptly in your conversation,"
said the graduate. "I want to tell you young
men a story. I have never told it before, and
would not tell it to any other audience, but I
know that it can be fully appreciated by you,
and it belongs to your traditions. So I am
going to give it to you, if you do not mind being bored for a while by an old grad."

" I don't think any of us will raise any serious objections," said Stoughton, as he paused.

The graduate smiled and then began : " As I said when I just now interrupted your discussion, there was another side to the glory of the war times in the old college. To the war itself there was, of course, another side, and I was on it. Up to the breaking of the storm we boys had not troubled ourselves much about the outlook. Most of us took politics lightly, and though burning then, still, among us at least, they were, as now I suppose, more the subject of good-natured chaff than of bitter feelings. However deeply the more thoughtful of us may have felt, they never allowed their convictions to interfere with their friendships. Of course, there were a few loud-mouthed zealots who made themselves disagreeable, but they were as much so to men of their own opinions as to those of the opposite.

" Hardly any one really expected war, or, if he did, ever said so. The historic shot fired on Sumter was, therefore, as much of a shock to our little community as to all of the North— even more, for a civil war meant more to us. To us, you know, fraternity is a reality.

" When the news came so that it could not be denied, it was not talked of between us Southerners and the rest. Next came the news that my State had gone out. That night my chum Jim Standish and I sat in our window-seat and smoked a long time without speaking. Finally the question came from him, ' Well, old man, are you going ? ' I said, ' Yes.' Then he put out his hand and I took it hard. When we had nearly finished our pipes Jim spoke again, ' When this is over, Tom,' he said, ' you will come back and get your degree with us.' I shook my head, I remember, and answered : ' It won't be over until long after our commencement—or else Harvard will be in a country foreign to me.'

" You see I remember that evening and the conversation very vividly. It was all we ever held on the subject. I knew what Jim's opinions were, and he knew mine well enough ; but he was too much of a gentleman to make my position any harder for me than it was. I was going to do what I considered my duty,—let that pass now also ; it was more than a quarter of a century ago.

" Very soon the letter came from home, but I

did not need it to hurry me. Jim and I were together almost every minute until I went away, and all my other friends seemed to go out of their way to show me courtesy and affection.

"The night before I left was Strawberry Night at the Pudding, and I remember I had intended not to go to the rooms. They were then in the top of Stoughton. I was packing in my room when Jim and Harry Rodes and one or two others came in, as a committee, to insist on my going. The committee accomplished its purpose by the usual smooth-tongued diplomacy of the undergraduate. They told me not to make a damn fool of myself, and that if I did not come round like a man, the theatricals should not go on. So I went, and tried to forget on my last night in the Yard that there was any world outside of it. That is the play-bill of those theatricals hanging over there on the wall now. What a time we had that night!

"I went home next day, with Clayton Randolph, Jack Randolph's father, as the rising generation always puts it. There was not much difficulty in getting South at that time.

I enlisted soon after I arrived, and, as a result, was rather busy for four years.

"Of course, for a long time I heard nothing from Cambridge. You boys know how almost the whole graduating class went to the front, and many an underclassman did not wait for his Commencement. You can read the degrees won by some of them in Memorial Hall. Every now and then I saw in that precious booty, a Northern newspaper, a name that I had last heard called in a recitation, or had myself many a time shouted across the Yard.

"The stray Northern papers were not my source of news in all cases. There was one name that for a time was in the mouths of all our men, and I had to risk their scorn and suspicion in defending it. They would hardly believe that the man who could lead a black regiment, and die in the front of his niggers in that terrible charge on Fort Wagner, was not a hardened ruffian, a desperate mercenary, but a fair-haired boy of five-and-twenty, and the most sunny, lovable gentleman that ever left the ballroom for the battle-field.

"I saw myself the fall of a man of different mould, but of the same metal. We were hold-

ing a strong position and had repulsed two
heavy charges, when we saw the enemy form-
ing for a third. This time they came closer
than in either of the previous attempts, and it
looked for a minute as if they would reach us.
But our fire was frightful, aided by several
batteries that were pouring in grape and canis-
ter at short range. The regiment immediately
in front of us came on well; but no body of
men could stand it, and at last it wavered and
then broke. Through the smoke I could see
a mounted officer tearing about and trying
desperately to rally the men, striking with the
flat of his sword, and evidently beside himself
with anger. Then, as he found it was no use
and his men left him, he turned, rode all alone
straight at us, and was shot through and
through. I have seen too much of what is
ordinarily called courage to be attracted to a
man solely by that commonest of virtues; but
this man's splendid scorn of surviving his failure,
his fury at what he considered disgrace, and his
deliberate self-sacrifice, lifted his act above the
common run of bravery. That man had breeding, and I wanted to have a look at him,
After the fight was over, I went to where he

lay dead with his horse. It was Boredon of
'61. I had hated that man. He had been one
of those disagreeable cranks of whom I have
spoken, a man absorbed with one idea and
allowing that idea to color all his feelings, and
spoil his manners. He had been to me as a
red rag to a bull. But when I recognized him
there, I would have given a great deal to have
been able to tell him how proud I was of him.
Evidently he had at least the hard part of a
gentleman. I went back to my brother officers.
and, with a good deal of boyish swagger I am
afraid, said to them, ' That fellow was at Harvard with me. That is the sort of fools they
make there.'

" Well, the war went on until we were hemmed
in around Richmond in '64. It was at that
time that I ran across Clayton Randolph, whom
I had not seen since we left Cambridge together. I came near not recognizing him in
the circumstances in which I found him. A
battery of artillery had got stuck in the mud,
but as I came up to it the last gun was being
dragged out. An officer seemed to be doing
most of the work, shoving on the wheels and
encouraging his tired men. Shortly afterwards

we were again halted next to the same battery, and there was the same officer sitting on a stump. His old uniform was covered with mud and axle-grease; his beard was four days' old; but he was Clayton Randolph, Randolph the dandy, Randolph, the model of neatness, whose perfect clothes had always been an object of chaff among us; Randolph, whose heaviest labor had been to polish his hat, and deepest thought to plan a dinner. He was sharing his piece of stale cornbread with a hungry little darky. You may imagine that we were rather glad to see each other. Clayton, however, had no more Cambridge news to give me than I had to give him, which was rather a disappointment. His battery was stationed near my regiment that winter, so we managed to see a good deal of each other in camp.

" One day, as I was sitting in front of my tent, I saw Clayton come galloping into the company street as though carrying urgent despatches. On seeing me he began shouting and waving his cap, as if there was danger that I might not see him and hear what he had to say. He was evidently beside himself about something,—and so was I, when he pulled up and yelled: 'What do you think? Jim Standish is in Libby prison!'

"I forget how he had learned this, but I remember he was very sure of it. By great luck and much energy we both managed to get leave that same day, and go to Richmond together; but we were disappointed in our hopes of seeing Jim. We turned every stone we could, and tried our best with the authorities, but it was no use; we could not get into the prison. There had been several escapes at that time, and no visitor of any sort was allowed to enter. The provost in charge, however, who knew Clayton, told us we might send Jim a letter, subject, of course, to its examination by the authorities. So we wrote him that we were there, and asked if there was anything he wanted us to send him. We explained that we could not get in to see him, but that he must write us all the news he could.

"In a short time the guard who had taken our note came back and asked what relation to us 'that young feller' was. We told him no relation by blood, but something a little closer, perhaps. 'Well,' said he, 'I never saw a feller take on so when I give him your note. He begged me to let him talk to you, and he most cried. Then he begged worse kind just to let him look out of a window where he could see you. He asked which side of the house you was on, and I reckon if I'd ha' told him he'd ha' made a break for the window and risked my shootin' him. I was right sorry, but I could n't do nothin' for him but get him some paper. He's writin' you a letter now, and says for you to be sure and wait for it.'

"There was no danger of our not waiting for it. Neither of us had heard a word from the old place or from any of our friends for three years. I suppose none of you boys has ever been separated from his college friends for a longer time than the long vacation?"

"I was away for a year after graduating," answered Dane Austin. "I was abroad with a classmate, and I remember the first long letter from one of our chums; all about the Springfield game, and what all 'the gang' were doing. We read that letter over every day for a month."

"Then you can imagine what it was to get news after three years, and three such years. We waited and waited for that letter, and at

last it came out to us—a regular volume. I
have it now. I don't believe Jim ever wrote so
much in all his college work put together. We
sat with our backs against a wall while I read it
aloud.

" First it gave us all the news from Cambridge ;—among other things, that we had won
the boat-race on Lake Quinsigamond. Randolph said that almost made up for Gettysburg,
and we had a little cheer all to ourselves. I
remember a man came running up to hear what
the news was and whether the Yankees had
been licked anywhere. We told him not that
we knew of, but Harvard had beaten Yale, and
he went off damning us for making such a row
about nothing. The letter went on to say that
there would probably be no race that year, as
most of the rowing men had gone off to the
war. Almost all of our old set had gone into
the army, it said. That jolly, good-for-nothing
rattle, bad Bob Bowling, who was always on the
ragged edge of expulsion, always in hot water
with the Faculty, and who had been booked by
every one for a very bad end, had disappointed
them all and found a distinguished career in a
cavalry regiment. But the hero of the class

was little Digges, 'Nancy' Digges, the quiet,
shy, little pale-faced student who looked as if
he would blow away in a strong wind, and
whom no one had thought was good for anything but grubbing for Greek roots.   This man
had been promoted several times for gallantry.
At Gettysburg, when Longstreet's corps was
right on top of his battery, when his supports
had been driven in, his horses shot, and his
gunners were falling around him, he had
dragged his guns back by hand, one by one,
and stopped to spike the last while one of our
men was reaching for him with a bayonet.
When I read this we both exclaimed : 'Well,
I 'll be hanged, Little Nancy ! ' "

   " It was at Gettysburg also that Jim had seen
Harry Rodes.   The last time that Jim had seen
him before that was just before leaving college,
when Rodes had been elected president of the
Hasty Pudding ; this time he was lying in the
grass, where it was red.   There was like news
of several other old chums.

   " ' As for your humble servant,' Jim wrote,
'he has only succeeded in getting himself ig-
nominiously jugged by your Johnnies.' I heard,
long afterwards, how he had been captured, pin-

ned under his dead horse, with a broken sabre, and three of our men to his score. ' This is not so much fun,' he went on, 'as that night in the Newton jail, which perhaps you may remember, Tom. You got me into that, you riotous companion and perverter of my youth.' I remembered that scrape of our Sophomore year very well, but I had a strong impression that it was Jim who upset the officer of the law. He told us he could stand Libby, however, well enough, if he only had a little smoke, and asked if we could not give aid and comfort to the invader in the shape of tobacco. At this Randolph exclaimed : ' Jim Standish without his pipe ! That is a real case of suffering among the prisoners !' The letter wound up with an injunction to answer it at once and tell all about ourselves and the other boys on our side, and with the hope that we should all be at the next triennial dinner.

" As soon as we had read the letter we went off and spent all our savings in tobacco. That was the only cheap thing in Richmond in those days, and we got enough to last Jim for months, though I have no doubt that he at once gave most of it away. Then we got some paper, and wrote him all we knew of the Harvard men on our side of the fence. We could give an equally good account of them, too ; for though, as disobedient children, Alma Mater has frowned on us, she never had cause to blush. We finished the letter before it was time for us to go back to camp, and sent it with the tobacco to Jim. We promised to try again to see him, but neither of us could get leave for a long time. If we had there would have been little chance of our getting into Libby ; and if we had gotten into Libby, we should not have found Jim there."

As the speaker paused Stoughton asked, " Why? did he es——" and then stopped, inwardly cursing himself, as he noticed a look that was coming into the face of the narrator. But the latter at once relieved him immensely by continuing.

" Yes, he escaped—very soon after our visit. A lot of prisoners got out together, Jim among them. The news was sent to all the troops near Richmond and instructions to keep a sharp lookout for them. Jim managed to get to our very outer lines, and one pitch-dark night tried to run the picket. The officer in command saw him in the brush and challenged him. Jim, trusting to the darkness and his old hundred-yard records, tried to make a dash for it. The officer fired and shot—shot him down like a dog."

The speaker's cigar had apparently gone out, and no one looked at him while he relit it. They looked at the walls where the firelight danced over the rollicking play-bills of thirty years ago. In a moment the graduate spoke again :

"As I leaned over the dearest friend I ever had, we recognized each other and he smiled. I took his head in my lap and he died holding my hand."

" Then you saw him before he died ? Were you with the picket ? " asked Gray.

" Yes.—I commanded the picket."
10

IT was all the result of a violent discussion in Stoughton's room. Hudson held that four miles an hour was an easy walking gait; Stoughton and Gray said it was n't.

"I tell you," said the latter, "when you are doing better than three and a half, you are hitting it up pretty well, and you could n't keep it up for any length of time. Don't you remember, Dick, we timed ourselves when we walked out from Boston the other night? It took us fifty minutes from the corner of Charles and Cambridge Streets, and that is just about three miles."

"Yes, and we went at a pretty good pace too," added Stoughton.

"That was probably after a supper at Billy Parks'," Hudson explained; "under those circumstances you undoubtedly covered a great many more miles than the crow flies between here and Boston."

" No, witty youth, it was n't anything of the kind. We don't follow in your footsteps," retorted Dick to this innuendo. " No, sir, you could n't walk four miles an hour all day to save your neck."

" I 'm betting I could," Hudson replied, " I have done it often out shooting."

" I dare say you thought so ; have you ever tried it over a measured stretch ? "

" No, but I can guess at about what rate I am walking, and four miles an hour is a good easy swing. I 'll bet you a V that I can do twenty-four miles in six hours."

" I 'll take that," answered Stoughton, promptly.

" So will I, if you offer the same," said Gray.

" Yes, I 'll bet with you, too," said Hudson.

Just at that moment Ned Burleigh came in, going through the form of giving the door a thump as he opened it, and telling himself to come in.

" What are you abandoned sports betting about now ? " he asked, as he covered the whole front of the fireplace as usual.

" Steve thinks he can walk twenty-four miles in six hours," answered Stoughton, " and we each have five dollars worth of opinion that he can't. What do you think about it?"

"I don't know; he is a pretty fast young man. Is it to be on a cinder track, or over an ordinary road? That would make a great difference."

"Have you any fond hope," asked Hudson, "that I am going to make a Roman holiday of myself on Holmes' Field for the edification of you children and the whole University? I am quite aware that that is just what you would like ; you would be out there with a brass band. No, my friend, I ask for no advantages. I am quite willing to take my chances over any ordinary country road, and in ordinary clothes."

"Extraordinary English knickerbockers, you mean," corrected Ned.

"You can take the road from here to Framingham," suggested Stoughton. "That is a perfectly straight one and you can't miss it. It is a little short of twenty-four miles, but we will allow you the slight difference."

"Yes, I know that road," said Hudson. "I drove over it when I was at school at Southborough. Strike the Worcester turnpike, don't you, after crossing the river at Watertown, and then keep on through Newton, Wellesley, Natick, and all those places? All right, I 'll take that road.

Ned Burleigh reflected a moment. " I think," he admitted, with a shake of his head, " that it can certainly be done by any man with strength and sand ; but Steve Hudson can't do it."

" I 'll tell you what, old fatty-cakes," declared Hudson, indignantly, " I 'll bet *you ten* dollars on the event."

" No, I won't go you ten, because I don't believe in betting so much on a certainty. Besides, you are hard up now, and you would undoubtedly borrow from me the money with which to pay me your bet. I can't afford to have you do that, sweet me child, but I will contribute a five like the others, towards this purse."

It was arranged that Hudson should choose his day, and give notice of it to the others in the morning. Then the tones of the ancient bell, tolled by the ancient Jones, came from the ancient belfry of Harvard Hall, and Hudson and Gray went over to a recitation in University Hall.

When they had gone Burleigh delivered himself of a great whoop of ecstasy. " He can do it easily, I know," he said. "We shall lose our money, but, Great Cæsar, it will be worth the admission. We must get all the others to bet with him, too, so that he won't back out. Let's go and get ready for it at once."

" What do you mean?" queried Stoughton, " what are you going to do?"

" Can't you guess, Mack, you Eyetalian? Come on, I'll tell you," and they went out over the Square towards a printer's.

Three or four days after this Hudson appeared at breakfast in his walking breeches and big Scotch stockings and announced he was going to start. He would leave Harvard Square at half-past ten o'clock and arrive at the town hall in Framingham at half-past four on that afternoon.

Stoughton and Gray said that they might be at the finish to receive him, if they found nothing better to do, otherwise he could time himself at the finish. Both of these men had ten o'clock lectures, so they could not see him start. Holworthy and Randolph had promised to make up a four for a morning pull on the

river. Rattleton, of course, had not yet come
to breakfast. Burleigh also had a ten o'clock
that he felt he really ought not to cut (it did
not strike Steve at the time that this was no
reason to Ned for not cutting); so he regretted
exceedingly that he would have to let Steve
start off uncheered and time himself. He would
endeavor to be at the finish, however, to carry
Hudson home.

Promptly at half-past ten Steve left Haryard
Square, with a swinging stride, and struck up
Garden Street by the Washington elm and
thence to Brattle Street. He was in fine form
and spirits and had chosen his day well. It was
one of our glorious, manful November days that
have had much to do, I firmly believe, with the
progress of this nation ; days when a man can
do anything; when the sparkling, drinkable
Northwester floods your lungs, and swells your
chest into a balloon that seems to lift you clear
of the ground. On such a day the twenty-four
miles ahead of him seemed nothing to Hudson, and he sprang along overflowing with
spirits.

The historic University town, with all its as-
sociations, seemed to him more beautiful and

interesting than ever. Washington, he thought, might have taken command of an army under the old tree four or five times a day in such weather. No wonder Longfellow could keep the Muse at his fireside in that fascinating Craigie house. As he neared the end of Brattle Street, he went by peaceful Elmwood, where a poet, ambassador, scholar, and patriot was then ending his days ; and buoyant, youthful Steve was struck by that perfect waiting-place for the great gentleman whose work was done. He wondered whether any of *his* friends would ever stir and honor the nation, and whether the great man had been anything like them when he was a fool undergrad. The traditions of the Hasty Pudding said that he had been a good deal like other boys.

Hudson reached Watertown well ahead of time. To his annoyance he saw that the street through which he had to pass was crowded, principally with small boys. "Something or other must have happened," he thought. "A dog-fight, or a runaway, or a man carried into a drug store. If the attraction is still on, I am all right ; if not, I shall have to run the gauntlet."

He soon discovered that the latter apprehension was the true one, and that he was in for just that species of entertainment. A great cheer went up as he approached, and a body of embryo leading citizens ran forward to meet him. They closed in all around and escorted him along the main street between two lines of shouting people.

"Hey, mister, give us some!" "Go on, you'll do it; good boy, Wingsey." "When 're yer goin' to fork 'em out?" "Rats, dat ain't him, dat fancy guy is one o' de Ha'vards, sure." "Will yer look at de jay?" "Get on to de legs!" "What 's he got 'em wrapped up in, shawls?" "Naw, carpets." "Say, mister, yer pants is got caught inside yer socks." "I guess them is English, yer know." "Ain't yer going to give us no gum?" "A—ah, let 'm alone, he ain't nothin' but one o' them stoodent jays. He ain't no winged wonder, a—ah!"

The above was what Steve enjoyed in his progress through Watertown. He finally shook off his pursuers on the edge of the village, and breathed freely again, as he "crossed the river and mounted the steep." The beauty of the Charles begins at this point, and he sat down

for a minute to look at it and rest.   On his left
was the first dam, the end of navigation for the
college craft; on his right the river wound
away from its high banks to the brown meadows
beyond.   While he sat there a four-oared crew
shot under the bridge and rested on their oars
in the quiet pool at his feet, just in front of the
falls.   He knew the man who was steering
and called to him.   "Hullo, Hudson," came
the recognition, "what are you doing up
here?"

"Off on a tramp.   Glorious day for exercise,
is n't it?"

"Yes, you have no idea how I enjoy this
rowing," answered the coxswain.

"Have you seen Holworthy and Randolph
up around this part of the river?"

"No, they were coming in this boat, but
backed out because they had something else
on hand, I believe."

"Oh, did they?   Well, good-by, I have got
to hurry along.   I am walking against time."

Steve strode on through Newton, and Newton
Centre, and Newton Lower Falls, and all the
other Newtons, and to his horror he found in
each town the same gathering, and went through

the same ovation that he had received in Watertown. Had he gone to work and picked out a
public holiday? No, he was sure it was not that,
and the fact that it was Saturday, and the schools
had therefore turned their swarms loose on the
suffering country, would not account for all of
the crowd in every village. Perhaps there was
an extra election going on in that county.
What puzzled him most, however, was that all
the urchins seemed to expect something of
him besides mere amusement, and a pitiable
example of dress.

He passed close by Joe Lee's at Auburndale;
several children ran across the lawn of the
famous hostel, and after " sizing him up," went
back with expressions of disappointment. The
worst trial of all, however, was the battery at
Wellesley. He had to go by the Female College, or Ladies' Seminary, and there was a large
group of the students of that institution, by the
roadside. Steve had never before been afflicted
with bashfulness, and did not acknowledge that
he was troubled in that way now, but he felt
peculiarly alone, and would have given much
for another man or just a few less girls. By the
terms of his bet he could not run any of the

distance ; but a giggle almost made him throw
up the stakes and break the pace.　By a great
effort, however, he brazened it out, and even
smiled cheerfully.　He made a penitent inward
resolution never to lean out of the window
again when a girl went through the Yard.

When more than half way, he stopped to
speak with a farmer leaning over the fence by
the road.　The uncrossed Yankee of the rural
districts still clings to a prejudice of his fathers,
a prejudice, long since dropped in our more
progressive communities, that a man has a right
to wear what he chooses and do what he chooses
provided he neither shocks nor interferes with
any one else.　This old farmer looked at Steve
with wonder and interest, but did not think it
necessary, as had the good citizens of the factory
towns, to heap scorn and derision on "de
dood."　He bowed to the wayfarer, as he would
to any well-behaved stranger.

"Good afternoon," said Hudson, grateful for
this drop of human kindness.　"Can you tell
me, sir, how far it is to Framingham?"

"Wa–al, abaout nigh on to ten mile or more,
they call it.　There 's a train goes pretty soon ;
ye won't find it so fur in the cars."

"Oh, I 'm going to walk it," explained Steve, with a smile.

"Thet 's a powerful long walk, young man. How fur ye come already?"

"From Cambridge."

"Gosh! Well your legs is young and pretty long, but ye must want suthin to do' pretty bad. Be ye broke or anythin'? Want any victuals?"

"No, thanks, I am walking for fun, trying to do it on time, you see."

"Mebbe you 're advertisin' suthin'? Oh, I want to know! Be you the winged wonder o' Westchester, or some sech place I hear tell on jest now?"

A light began to glimmer in Hudson's mind. He had been asked several times if he was the "winged wonder," but had paid no attention to the question, supposing that it was merely a form of the great public wit. Now it was asked him in perfect good faith, and the name of his own home was added to the alliteration. He began to connect his persecution with Holworthy and Randolph's failure to row.

"No," he answered his friendly interrogator, "not intentionally, but I am beginning now to suspect that I *am* occupying some such position. I am much obliged to you for your information. I must move along now."

" Good day, sir ; guess ye 'll want a heap o' corn-plasters when ye git to Framin'am."

" Not with these stockings," laughed Hudson, glad of an opportunity to justify his clothes, " they 're thick and soft, great things to walk in."

" They be, eh ? Well, I kinder thought they was n't just for looks. I don't want none to-day, though, good day."

" Good-by," and Steve went on, feeling sure that the old man still suspected him at least of peddling footgear.

Just before the end of his tramp he sat down for a rest on an inviting fence rail. He had plenty of time to spare, but the grassy bank might have kept him too long and made him stiff. Oh, how pleasant that three-cornered rail did feel! A piece of paper blew across the road and whirled up in his face. It was a hand-bill of some sort ; he remembered now having seen several of them along the way, but had picked up none. He caught this one and turned it over. This was what he read :

HE IS COMING!

WAIT FOR HIM! WATCH FOR HIM!

THE WINGED WONDER OF WESTCHESTER!

PEERLESS PEDESTRIAN PRODIGY!

He is matched to walk twenty-four miles to-day for an enormous purse. He holds world records for pedestrianism. He will wear one of our custom-made London suitings, unexcelled for natty outdoor wear and stylish appearance. They are all the rage in England, and therefore sure to be popular here.

He will also distribute, gratis, tops and marbles to the boys and chewing-gum to the ladies. Watch for him, everybody; he will be here soon, and will follow this road.

COME OUT, GIRLS! COME OUT, BOYS!
NOW IS YOUR CHANCE.

WAIT, WATCH FOR THE WINGED WONDER
OF WESTCHESTER!

The glimmer dawned to a great light. He jumped down and hurried along the remaining mile or two as fast as his weary legs would go.

There was no crowd awaiting him on the out-
skirts of Framingham, and for a few minutes
he hoped that he was going to at least finish in
peace. Vain hope ! As he approached the
public square he saw it crowded with people
and heard the strains of a brass band. On turning the corner he was received with a great
shout. Then he saw a sight that 'explained it
all, and caused him to exclaim, " The three-
year-old idiots ! "

In front of the town-hall was drawn up a
barge with four plumed horses. In it were a
band of music and a full delegation of Steve's
devoted friends. Ned Burleigh was up on the
box haranguing the populace.

" What sort of a fool circus are you children
trying to make of yourselves," asked Hudson,
as he came up.

" A grand one, old man, and you have been
the elephant, the shining star of the whole
show," replied Burleigh. " You will find beer
in the ambulance."

" You have won the money handsomely,
Steve," acknowledged Stoughton, " and we all
accept with pleasure your kind invitation to
dinner."

A RAMBLING DISCUSSION AND AN AD-
VENTURE, PERHAPS UNCONNECTED.

DICK STOUGHTON came to lunch that day in a decidedly bad humor, cause unknown. He was late, and all the other members of the club table were there, including the two dogs. A "Gray baiting" was going on. This sport consisted in working up the poetic feelings of Ernest Gray, and then ruthlessly harrowing the same. Gray was a fiery, imaginative little man, whose soul compassed far more than his body. His impulsive nature drove him constantly into the net spread by his friends, but he had become used to the process, and perhaps it did him good. Whether or not he had in him the stuff for a true poet, he was at least in no danger among those men of becoming a false one. He was just then stirred to a fine condition on the subject of Philistinism, was violently supporting the famous professor of the Humanities, and had almost got to the point of quoting poetry.

"It makes me laugh a low, sad laugh, " remarked Stoughton, gloomily buttering a muffin, "when I think what Gray will be doing thirty years from now."

"We have arranged all that," said Burleigh. "Ernest is going to marry a strong-minded woman four times as big as himself, who will take him out shopping and make him carry the bundles and the twins."

"No, it will be a greater change than that," continued Dick. "At fifty he will probably be a keen, representative business man. He will be celebrated for being better able than any one in Wall Street to cheat his neighbor, and he will be absorbed in the occupation. He will be a man of strength and stamen, a man of industry, a plain, hard-working man. He will publish Letters of a Parent, in bad English, about the degeneracy of education at Harvard, and will refuse to send his sons here for fear of their becoming dudes and loafers. He won't spoil good paper then with odes and fantasies; he will devote it, instead, to watering stock and foreclosing mortages. Just see if he does n't."

"Are you narrow enough to think," asked Gray, defiantly, "that a man cannot work in this world, and work hard, without shutting his mind to everything outside of his tool shop?"

" Perhaps he can," answered Stoughton, " but he never does in this country ; he has n't time. Whatever we take up, we have got to keep at fever heat or else go to the wall. It will be work, work, work until we become utterly un-interesting machines. It can't be helped, we have got to make up our minds to it some day and we had better do so now. We are all wasting four valuable years in this anomalous spot of Cambridge, when we ought to be learn-ing bookkeeping. We are a nation of one-sided workers, and we might just as well accept the situation philosophically. I am sure I for one don't care a cent. Only I wish I had not fooled away my time so long, with a set of men made up of dilettantes and bummers."

Dick emphasized the concluding word by handsomely scooping the last sausage just ahead of Jack Randolph, who with a bow and wave of his hand gracefully acknowledged the defeat. It was a strict rule of etiquette at the club table to take the odd trick of any dish, whether you wanted it or not.

" Hello," exclaimed Burleigh, with a happy

light in his face, " Dick has waked up to the seriousness of life again. That is the third time this month." Stoughton's occasional pessimism was as fair game to his friends, as Gray's poetry, so the victim for that day's lunch was promptly changed.

" So he has," added Hudson. " He has a good, old-fashioned attack of remorse. Where were you last night, Dick? Must have been an awful spree."

" Is it a letter from your governor?" queried Rattleton, sympathetically.

" Perhaps it is the letter on your forensic," suggested Randolph. " Jack Rat got an E. on his, but just see how sweetly *he* takes it."

" A little serious reflection is undoubtedly a good thing for you, my son," observed Hollis Holworthy. " But though I don't want to flatter you, excuse my saying that you talk like an ass. Even if your premises were true your conclusion is false. If we Americans are all such narrow-minded money-makers, that is all the more reason for trying to be something better. But it is n't so. I don't believe work has necessarily any such effect. Gray is right."

" My conclusion is all right. The difference

between us is that I am perfectly contented to be as the rest of my countrymen are ; you want to be something different, *ergo*, you are a snob. Furthermore my premises *are* true, and you will find them so, my poor children. I am a few years in advance of you, that's all. Just see how men change after they leave college. Go over to the Law School and look at those grinds, each one working night and day to get ahead of the rest. I met old Dane Austin the other day crossing the Yard, three huge books under each arm, and a pair of spectacles across his nose. He used to be the best built man in the 'Varsity boat, but he does n't touch an oar now, and won't try for the crew, unless they absolutely need him at the last minute. He is getting red-eyed and pale, and looks almost hollow-chested. A man can't keep up with the law and pay any attention to his physique. He is losing all his strength and good looks."

"You had better hit him once and find out," suggested Holworthy.

" Thanks ; I don't care to put my theories to quite such a test," acknowledged Dick, with a grin. " But it is true just the same. It is true of every other occupation. Go down to New

York and stand on Wall Street. You will see a dozen men you knew, at least by sight, in college, men who used to be well-dressed and well-bred. Down there they rush by you with a nod, in all sorts of costumes,—dirty, slovenly, nervous. Sometimes they will stop for a moment to shake hands, and make some impertinent remark on your clothes. I don't mind the prospect myself, but I am only laying it fairly before you blissful, careless, conceited youths."

"I rather think you will find that those fellows have n't forgotten how to turn themselves out properly when there is any need for it," said Holworthy. "You don't wear your town togs to recitations here."

"There is no doubt about it, this work and worry does spoil a man's looks," said Burleigh. "Just look at that poor wreck over there," pointing to Rattleton.

That student had finished his lunch (or breakfast) and stretched his legs as usual in the next chair. He was engaged in throwing crackers for his dog Blathers to catch, and was rather out of the conversation. He caught the last remark only.

"You have no idea what a handsome man I'd be if I did n't work so hard," he replied.

"It is all right for you, Jack," Stoughton went on. "A watchful Providence has sent you an income. It is almost a pity, though, for you would make a fascinating tramp. No amount of either starvation or public opinion would ever make you change your calm, philosophical life. But the rest of us must all get into the procession and keep up with the brazen band. No wonder so many of our girls marry Englishmen. They are dead right, too; they don't want to marry worn-out machines, they prefer men."

"Hurray!" shouted Hudson. "The secret is out. Some Englishman has cut him out with his best girl."

"I am not handicapped with any such nonsense, thank Heaven," growled Dick. "But if I was, by Jove, I would n't be fool enough to do any work for her sake, as so many misguided men do. No, sir, I'd take life easily and keep my figure, as our trans-Atlantic cousins do. I'd spend my days with the daughter and live on the old man. That is what girls like, and they do have some sense."

" That is perfect rot," exclaimed the poetic Gray, expressing his roused sentiment with more force than grace. " Life to-day is just what it was in the days of chivalry. A true knight must prove his love with his lance, and win his wife like a man."

" There you go, of course," answered Stoughton ; " clap your leg over Pegasus, and off across country, regardless of hedges and ditches, or the narrow roads of commerce. Suppose his lance got busted, as was frequently the case ? "

" Sic 'im, sic 'im " chuckled Burleigh. " We have got the poet and the cynic by the ears. Oh, this is lovely ! "

" Both of 'em amateurs," added Holworthy, " and neither knowing what he is talking about."

" Two to one on the poet, though," said Randolph. " He is always in earnest, anyway."

" Shake hands, gents," said Rattleton, getting interested. " Time."

" Now just listen to me," said Dick, tilting back his chair and waving his fork pedantically. " I 'll give you a really accurate picture of your dear days of chivalry, such as you never got out of a romance."

" Silence for Sir Walter Stoughton's account of a tourney," commanded Burleigh. "Steve Hudson, pull that pup of yours off the table; she 'll upset the milk pitcher."

" I have just been reading all about that sort of game," interrupted Rattleton. " Seems to me they were a most unsporting lot. They had no classes or handicaps; just lumped 'em all in together, feather-weights and heavy-weights. No idea of a fair thing."

" Shut up your childish prattle, Jack," commanded Burleigh. " If you will push your researches far enough you will find that the little fellows always won. The giants invari-ably got the heads smote off 'em. We are not on the brutal subject of prize-fighting, we are on chivalry. You know nothing about that, so keep quiet and let Dick go on."

" I suppose you have an idea," Stoughton went on, " that every interesting young gentle-man who entered the lists was a sure winner, and then all he had to do was to crown the heroine as Queen of Love and Beauty and live happily ever afterwards. Now of course that was n't so. Some one had to get thrashed, and most young knights probably occupied that position for the first ten years or so of their career. Take an individual case; Sir Ernest Gray, bent on winning glory for Dulcinea, looks over the sporting calendar and enters himself for every big field-meeting during the season. He bears himself right bravely in them all, but gets stood on his head with great regularity; in fact Dulcinea gets a little tired of watching his performance. Nevertheless she goes to the crack meeting of Ashby de la Zouche, to see Gray try again.

"This tourney is carried off with great ease by an old hand, Sir Thomas de Mainfort, who, having been separated from his third wife on the ground of brutal treatment, is not doing any love-proving with his lance. He is simply a mug hunter; he is in for the white Barbary steed, and the other fellows' armor."

"Gate money?" broke in Rattleton interrogatively.

"Same principle," answered Dick. "He wins the appointment of the Queen of Love and Beauty, and takes d—— good care to choose the king's elderly daughter; thereby putting in good work for a government office. Of course, none of the fair damsels in the ladies'

gallery are in the slightest degree interested in
him, that goes without saying ; but do you suppose that they are a bit more interested in the
poor youngsters whom he has been knocking
about ? Not much. The fellow who takes
their eyes is a chap in a white satin doublet,
cut in the latest French fashion, who has sent
flowers to Dulcinea, and is hanging over the
rail of the ladies' gallery, talking to her. He
is a delightful young man. He can sing the
songs of the Troubadours that he has heard
in Provence. He knows all the latest gossip
about that delicious row between the Pope and
the German Emperor. He spends the proper
season in each Continental court. He is so different from the homely, insular youths who
are pummelling each other down below in the
lists. They never can think or talk anything
but fight. He says funny things about those
youths, and criticizes their armor. Altogether
he is charming. Handsome and well preserved,
too. Splendid figure, and could undoubtedly
fight well if he had to ; but he does n't have
to, and is n't fool enough to do it. No bruises
on him.

"After the fight is over young Sir Ernest

comes along, in a sheepish sort of a way, to see
what Dulcinea thinks of his day's work. Sir
Ernest was a pretty good-looking boy when he
started on the career of arms. Now, however,
he is showing marks of wear. The saddle has
made him bow-legged, the helmet has worn off
much of his hair, and the gauntlet has raised
corns on his knuckles. Some of his front teeth
have been knocked out. Besides the wear and
tear in his personal appearance, his mind runs
largely on parries and thrusts, relative advantages of chain-mail and Milan plate, and all that
sort of shop talk. He can not sing the new
Romance songs, he knows only the old ones
that his nurse taught him. Dulcinea used to
like him very much, and is still fond of him in
a way. If he had accomplished the marvel of
winning the whole tournament, of unhorsing
the old veteran De Mainfort ; if he had won the
crown of Love and Beauty, and brought it to her,
giving that hideous stuck-up old Princess the
go-by, Dulcinea would have loved him fondly,
and been ready to marry him then and there.
But he has not brought her the crown of Love
and Beauty; he has only brought a stove-in
helmet and a black eye. True, he has been

fighting his level best, but how much good has it done him? He has unhorsed two or three young men of his own weight; he has even put up a stiff set-to against big De Thumper, who won the Templar stakes; but Dulcinea did not see him then, she was talking to the interesting foreigner. Then he ran up against Sir Thomas de Mainfort, and got landed on his back; Dulcinea was looking right at him that time. He got up like a little man, without claiming his ten seconds, and went for the redoubtable Sir Thomas again. Thereupon the big fellow smashed him on the jaw, and put him to sleep, so that it took his squires half an hour to bring him round. Dulcinea took that in, too, and the amusing foreigner remarked on what conceit a youngster must have to go in for this sort of thing against men like De Mainfort. The highest renown that the young knight has so far won may possibly be a line next day in the Ashby *Herald* and *Tournament Gazette.* It will run something like this: 'Where are we to look for the De Mainforts and Thumpers of the next generation? There is absolutely no new material worth mentioning. Young Gray gives a little glimmer of promise in some of his back-strokes, but his work is eminently crude and boyish. However, if he gets over his swelled head, he may in twenty or thirty years of hard work become a fair lance.' Do you think that helps his chances with Dulcinea? D—— that dog of yours, Hudson, she has stolen my muffin!"

"Are you all through?" demanded Gray, who had been restraining himself with difficulty.

"No; hold on. I have n't shown you half your trouble yet. At the banquet in the evening, Gray sits on one side of Dulcinea and the handsome stranger on the other. Gray is sore and tired and comes near falling asleep at the table, while the other fellow discusses the Italian painters, and tells anecdotes of the Dauphin of France. Gray used to be able to play the harp well, and can still play sometimes in the evenings, when his fingers are not too lame; but they generally are. He can also get into his satin doublet on Sundays and great occasions, and look almost as well as the other chap; but he does so *only* on occasions, whereas the stranger keeps himself up to the mark all the time. Dulcinea cannot help thinking, therefore, that Gray is a boor and a bore, even though he sometimes shows capabilites other than those of getting his head smashed. On the other hand, Dulcinea's governor is a stout baron of the old school. He looks upon Gray as a dude and aper of foreign customs, for taking a bath after a hard day in the lists and leaving off his breastplate at dinner. The old man's chief boast is that with his own good sword he has carved out all his fat lands and broad baronies, and he asks, as he proudly thumps his chest, how he could ever have done all that if he had put on effeminate airs and fooled away ten minutes every week in a bath-tub. Now I ask you to drop your poetry for a minute, substitute reason for imagination, and confess that this is really what a young knight had to take. Dixi, let 's hear what you have got to say."

"Just this," answered Gray, "that your Dulcinea is a fool. Any true woman would appreciate a man's best efforts, even if unsuccessful. I claim that such Dulcineas are the exception and not the rule. Point two. Your young knight is also a fool if he allows himself to become nothing but a mere bruiser and cutthroat. He ought not to forget that he is a gentleman as well as a fighting man. He can pay some attention to the graces of life and fight none the worse for it. You say he knows the old songs,—those are the best always—and he can pick up the new ones in spare moments. It makes no difference how he dresses, so long as he has a good excuse for dressing badly, and does n't forget how to dress well. As for your point about his personal appearace, that does n't amount to a row of pins. It certainly can't trouble him, and it would n't trouble Dulcinea if she had any sense. I don't believe any woman objects to honorable scars in a man."

" Every woman does n't throw poetry around them as you do. Honorable scars received in commonplace everyday scrapping don't count."

"This has not been a fair fight," declared Holworthy. "I can see through this man Stoughton, now, and understand it all. He has prepared all this harangue, and is trying to pass it off here as impromptu. Now, I am going to give him away. I was with him the other evening at a dinner. There was a girl there who had been abroad for the first time. She had spent the last season in London, for the expenses of which her governor probably had

to do double work at home. She had quite
naturally, fallen completely in love with all those
great big, splendid-looking chaps who float about
London in long coats all day during the season.
A handsome leisure class. Some of the biggest
and best dressed of them, by-the-way, are quite
apt to be her own humdrum countrymen on a
vacation, but she had n't found that out yet,
and it has nothing to do with the present discussion, anyway. I heard her remark to Dick
during dinner that Englishmen were so much
better looking and more agreeable than Ameri-
can men. That is an undeniable fact, in daily
life, but Dick was fool enough to get a little mad
over the observation. He could n't think of
any brilliant repartee at the time, but came
home and slept over it. Next time he meets
that girl, or one like her, he will be loaded for
bear, but he wants to rehearse a little, first, so he
has brought his mediæval metaphor here to try
it on the dog. He knew that our hair-trigger
poet, with a little joggling, would be morally
certain to shoot off something about love and
lances; that was just the opening he wanted.
Keep it for your next dinner-party, Dick. It
does n't mean anything but it may make you

12

feel clever and entertaining. I hold that Brother Gray has thrown you and your Dulcinea down hard."

"It is perfectly true to life, anyway," said Dick, with a conscious grin ; " but you are wrong in accusing me of worrying about it. I don't mind the prospect in the least, as I said before, and am only warning you snobs who think you are something pretty nice. You can't carry your poetry out of college. Your 'graces of life ' as you call 'em, either mental or physical, won't raise your salary in an office, and your hard work in the office won't help you to figure in a ballroom. If you get to the top before you are thirty, Dulcinea may smile on you ; but you are not likely to do anything of the kind. You will probably spoil all your other chances with her in the attempt."

"Listen to our man of the world, you fellows," said Burleigh. " Jack Rattleton, stop playing with that ugly pup and improve your advantages. Uncle Richard, here, aged two and twenty, has upon half a dozen occasions made the exertion of going to a party in Boston, where he has talked foot-ball with some *débutante* and been floored on Esoteric Buddhism by an elderly lady who had it. He has spent all the rest of his time smoking a villanous pipe in Cambridge. He is now giving us, from his wealth of experience, a few opinions and straight tips on the nature of woman."

· "I don't pretend to know anything about 'em," protested Dick, stoutly, "and care less. But this I do know, that, among most men, success counts for more than endeavor, and I am willing to bet that it is four times as much so with women."

"And I know this," said Hudson, "that you, on your own confession, don't know what you are talking about, and are in a beastly humor. You need exercise; come on over to Fresh Pond and go skating."

"Yes, do take him off," sighed Rattleton; "when he and Hol and Gray get theorizing it gives everybody a headache. They'll go around to the Pud. and keep it up there if you don't take them skating."

Stoughton replied to this by kicking the hind legs of Rattleton's carefully balanced chair, and upsetting him on top of the dog Blathers. After which exchange of courtesies the party adjourned, arranging to meet and go to Fresh Pond at three.

Holworthy did not join the skating party; he

had promised to go for a walk with his chum Rivers. Gray also had some engagement. As the others were starting out with their skates, they met the latter little gentleman arrayed in his best. He tried to pretend that he did n't see them. They promptly set up a cheer and began ostentatiously making snow-balls.

" Did n't you say something at lunch about men in New York who made impertinent remarks about your clothes," demanded Gray of Stoughton.

"This is n't New York," answered Stoughton. "When a man puts on all his feathers and paint on a week day in Cambridge, we know he is on the war-path."

" Dog his trail, dog his trail," yelled Hudson. "Let 's see what wigwam it leads to."

"Does n't he look pretty?" shouted Burleigh. " Only his coat does n't fit in the back."

"Look at that smooch on his collar," exclaimed Randolph.

"I hope you children will grow up sometime," grumbled Gray, as he hurried on.

An hour or two afterwards Gray was walking into Boston in very good company. The new Harvard Bridge was not then built, and the two (yes, only one other) were passing through one of the more lonely streets of Cambridge-port that lead to the Cottage Farms bridge. A hard-looking citizen turned a corner ahead of them, and on catching sight of the pair stopped with some insulting remark. Gray's blood boiled into his face, but he had sense enough to cross to the other side of the street with his convoy. The man, evidently in liquor, promptly did the same, and showed that he meant to give trouble.

" Run back as fast as you can to Main Street," said Gray to his companion, upon which advice she wisely and quickly acted.

The rough started forward, and Gray placed himself in the middle of the path.

" Hold on," he commanded. " Don't come a step nearer."

"Get out of my way, you little dude, before I eat you up," answered the other.

The little dude naturally did not get out of the way. He dropped his stick and squared himself for the enemy. Then, contrary to the generally accepted pleasant idea, the burly ruffian proceeded to "eat up" the slender thoroughbred.

The light-weight met his adversary's rush handsomely, but utterly failed to stop it. The tough closed, "back-heeling," and at the same time landing his right with a door key in it, used as brass knuckles, thereby cutting Gray's face open. As the latter tripped and went down under the blow, the tough kicked him. Gray jumped to his feet again, however, and managed to fasten on the rough's back as he went by. They went down together, the rough on top with his knee on Gray's stomach. This knocked the wind out of the little fellow terribly, still he clung to his adversary. The latter struggled to free one of his hands, with the amiable purpose of choking, or of gouging the eye of the youth under him, when a shout made him look up. He managed to tear himself away, and sprang to his feet. Holworthy and his chum, Charles Rivers, who was No. 4 in the 'Varsity crew, were tearing down the street.

The second battle was quite as unequal as the first, for there was as much difference between the big college oarsman in the pink of condition, and the rum-soaked Port tough, as there had been between the latter and the plucky little stripling. It is only justice to the tough, however, to say that no idea of flight entered his mind ; he was quite as ready to fight the big dude as the little one.

His hand went to his hip-pocket, but evidently the weapon was not there. Then he gathered himself and made a spring at the newcomer. As a result he ran his face into a big fist at the end of a long, straight, stiffened left-arm. At the other end of that arm were a hundred and ninety pounds of hard-trained muscle. As he staggered back from this concussion, he got the hundred and ninety pounds again, concentrated in a right hander on his fifth rib. That doubled him up, and then it was River's turn to rush. He knew enough not to close, for the brute, though practically knocked out, could still use his teeth if he got a chance. Holding him up by the throat with his left hand, with his right Rivers pounded the ruffian on the jaw, then threw him senseless on the ground.

" There, that will do. He 'll come to after awhile," he remarked, " but he will do no more mischief at present. You chivalrous little jackass," he continued, turning to Gray, who was wiping the blood from his face, " I saw you throw away your stick when we first caught sight of you. It 's lucky you were n't killed. Of course you could n't help fighting under these circumstances, but if you ever get caught with a beast like that again, don't ever try fair prize-ring methods with him. It is only in books that the nice young man thrashes two or three toughs bigger than himself in a square fight. These chaps know how to fight just as well as you ; what is more, they know how to fight foul, and always do if they get a chance. Just remember, now, if you ever have to tackle this kind of cattle again, cut him right over with your stick. Paste him under the ear for keeps."

"If this is n't just my luck!" said Gray, looking ruefully at the blood on his handker-chief. " Here have I been longing and praying for this sort of an opportunity, and when it comes, by Jove, I get a thundering licking and another fellow comes along and saves me and the girl both. Hang it, Charlie, I could have held on to him until she got away."

"Too bad," laughed Rivers, " I beg your pardon. I did n't think. I ought to have let you get killed or gouged for her and glory, ought n't I ? Come, cheer up, old man, you did a great deal more than I, and deserve all the favors. Let 's go back and see her."

They walked back to Holworthy and the fair *casus belli.* The latter had paused in her flight on the arrival of the reinforcements, and with natural curiosity and anxiety had watched the fray from a distance. As her rescued rescuer and his rescuer came up, she held out her hand to Rivers, and uttered her gratitude in nervous broken sentences.

She expressed much sympathy for Gray.

SERIOUS SITUATIONS IN BURLEIGH'S
ROOM.*

SCENE :—Room of Hudson, Burleigh, and Co. (Co. being
Topsy, the terrier).

Burleigh seated in easy chair, legs stretched towards fire,
back to table, dog in lap, reading and smoking long pipe.

Hudson [*from his bedroom*].   Oh, Ned !

Burleigh.   Hullo?

Hud.   Are n't you going to the Assembly
to-night ?

[*Enter Huason from bedroom putting on evening coat.*]

Burl. [*without looking up*].   Did you ever
know me to go to more than one Harvard
Assembly?   Don't ask foolish questions.

Hud.   Well, don't you be such a lazy lum-
mox.   [*Going to looking-glass.*]   Really, Ned,
you ought to go out more among decent
people.

Burl.   Yes.   I have such a good time when

* This farce is printed by the kind permission of the Hasty
Pudding Club for which it was originally written.

186

I do. At the last and only party in Boston to which I ever went, I knew just one girl, and spilled ice-cream on her dress. After holding up the wall for an hour and a half, and finding it impossible to get you or any one else to come back to Cambridge with me, I started home alone in Riley's cab. Mr. Riley felt in a sporting mood as usual, and insisted on racing an electric car. We broke down at Central Square. It was snowing hard and the walk home in patent leathers was lovely. When I got home, of course, I found that my keys were chained to my other trousers, and I busted the bags I had on in climbing through the ventilator over the door. I dropped on the rocking-chair and the pup both at once, and then found there was nothing to drink in the book-case. Oh, I enjoyed the last Assembly thoroughly. I think it would be fun to go again. Ugh!

Hud. Very few ever go to a party for pleasure, my dear boy. It is a duty that you owe to yourself. If you never go to balls, you will never know how to behave in a ballroom. When you have learned to do that, why then you need n't go to balls.

Burl. That is logical.

Hud. It is also a duty that you owe society.

Burl. Society can have my share of the supper, and call it square.

Hud. Well, now look here, Ned, I want you to go in to the Assembly to-night for a particular reason, besides your own civilization.

Burl. I won't go. What is your reason?

Hud. My mother and sister have come on to Boston and are going to be at the ball to-night, and I want you to meet them.

Burl. Why did n't you say that in the first place? But, Steve, are n't you going to have them out here pretty soon? I can meet them then.

Hud. [*emphatically*]. No, sir. Not if I know it, until I can be sure of keeping out all the duns and sporting gentry who are apt to call unexpectedly. Numerous acquaintances, whom I do not care to have my good mother meet, might drop in to a little five o'clock tea. I shall probably get my quarter's allowance before long, and then I can chain up the Furies for a while, and have my family out here with an easy mind. That bull mick Shreedy is gunning for me just at present, and if my mother knew I owed money to a prize-fighter she would never get over it.

Burl. Well, won't it do if I go in to-morrow and call?

Hud. No, I promised them that you would be there to-night, and they will be awfully disappointed if you 're not. They are naturally anxious to know my chum as soon as possible.

Burl. Then they will be awfully disappointed if I *am* there. You know perfectly well, when I talk to a girl at a party, what a painful ordeal it is for both of us. You ought not to spring me on your sister under such conditions. It 's unfair to me and a poor joke on her.

Hud. Oh, don't be such a bashful ass. You can do well enough if you try. My sister knows that you hate parties, and will appreciate your coming. Now, do promise me, there is a good fellow.

Burl. Well, I suppose I shall have to. But, Steve, I have n't time to dress for this thing to-night.

Hud. Nonsense. You have plenty of time to dress. How long does that operation generally take you?

Burl. Three quarters of an hour to dress, and an hour and three quarters to tie my cravat. I think I shall have to get one of those nice store cravats that come all tied, and strap on with a buckle.

Hud. Yes, get a pretty satin one with pink rose-buds on it. Oh, I should n't be surprised to see you turn up in anything. [*Putting on hat and overcoat.*] I tell you what it is, Ned, if you continue to shun all feminine society you will soon become an unmitigated boor.

Burl. I am at college, thanks, and prefer it. I shall have plenty of time to take up feminine society, as you call it, after I graduate.

Hud. You will be a cub, and society won't take *you* up. Now, old man, it is awfully good of you to come in on my account to-night, so don't back out,—and make yourself look as much like a gentleman as you can. Come in as early as possible.   [*Exit Hudson.*]

Burl. [*sol.*]. Why the deuce does a fellow want to go chasing into Boston, when he has only four years of this sort of thing. Steve does not half appreciate college. However, I suppose if his family [*Taking photograph from table*] is going to be there, I ought to go in. It is only decent. [*To photograph.*] So, Miss Hudson, you and I are going to meet, eh? Oh, what a fool you will think me! Now, if I could

nly look at you without trying to talk. Steve
right, though; I ought to cure myself of this
ool shyness and awkwardness before the other
ex, or I deserve to be called an ill-bred cub.

[*Knock at hall door.*]

Come in! [*Puts down photograph hastily.*]

Enter Jack Randolph in long coat and rubber boots.]

Randolph. Hullo, Ned! Did I leave my
mbrella in here the other day?

Burl. It is a pretty good one, is n't it? No,
guess I have n't seen it.

Rand. [*taking a cross-handled umbrella from
eside fireplace*]. Lucky you have n't.

Burl. Oh, while I think of it, here is that X
owe you [*pulling bill out of pocket*].

Rand. Good man! Marvellous memory!
Remembered the wrong end of a debt. I am
lad you did, for I am devilish hard up just at
resent. [*Taking cigar from mantel-piece.*]

Burl. So is everybody at this time of year.
This is a great sacrifice on my part.

Rand. Don't give it to me now. Keep it
ntil to-morrow, won't you? [*Lights cigar.*]

Burl. Better take it while you can get it. I

shall have spent it next time we meet. Why don't you want it now?

Rand. Well, I will take it, just to relieve you. I have n't anything on but this ulster, which is not a good thing to put money in. You see, I am going round to a dress rehearsal at the Pudding.

Burl. Oh, that is why you are all bundled up on this clear night. Let us see your dress.

Rand. No, you will see it soon enough at the show to-morrow night. Where is Steve?

Burl. Gone in town to trip in the mazy.

Rand. The habitual dude! Oh, of course, the first Harvard Assembly comes off to-night. If it was not for this rehearsal I would go in and do the butterfly myself. What would hire you to go there, Charlie?

Burl. Give me back that ten dollars and I will go.

Rand. I don't believe you would; but I'd give you the ten dollars if I could be there to see you.

Burl. Well, if it will please you to know it, I *am* going in.

Rand. What! You going to a party! What has happened?

Burl. [*with dignity*]. Nothing. It is a duty that I owe to myself and society. If a man never goes to balls he will never know how to behave in a ballroom.

Rand. [*with derisive laughter*]. That is pretty good from you. Steve has evidently been giving you a lecture. Come now, Ned, choke that off and tell me honestly what is up.

Burl. Nothing, I tell you. If a man shuns all polite society, he will become an unmitigated boor.

Rand. If you don't drop that second-hand stuff of Hudson's, and tell me who the girl is, by Jove, I 'll tell every man in college about it, and it shall be a very amusing story before I get through with it, I promise you.

Burl. Well, you see—er—Steve's mother is going to be there and he wants me to meet her.

Rand. Oho! That is it, is it? Steve's *mother* is going to be there. Ha-ha-ha, that is pretty weak, old fox. I suppose, of course, there is no chance of *Miss* Hudson being there too. Well, if she is half as pretty as her photograph, I don't blame you for going in. Egad, though, Ned, I would like to see you talking to her.

Burl. I have no doubt you would, sweet

13

me child, but you won't. That is just where
the best point of this funny joke comes in.
While I am talking to Miss Hudson, you will
be out here, at the rehearsal, getting sworn at.
"Go over that chorus again."   " Randolph,
you 're out of step."

Rand. Damn the rehearsal. Never mind,
Miss Hudson will probably be on here for some
time, and I shall get another chance of meeting
her.   When I do, I will make a particular point
of cutting you out. You won't be in it, even
if you are her brother's chum.

Burl. [*getting up*]. You are talking too
much. Come now, run along. I have got to
dress.

Rand. I wish I had time to watch you do
it. I don't believe you have put on a claw-
hammer coat since you 've been up here, except
for club dinners.

Burl. Oh, go round to your rehearsal. You
will be late.

Rand. [*going to hall door*]. If it does n't
begin on time, I 'll come back here and help
you untangle your neck-tie. Don't make yourself too pretty. Leave me some chance with
Miss H.   [*Exit.*]

Burl. Jack is too fresh to-night. Come, pup. [*Picks up Topsy and exits into bedroom.*] ·

[*Enter a certain Prof. Shreedy (unattached to the University.) He softly closes door after him, and knocks on inside*].

Burl. [*from bedroom*]. Come in.

Shreedy [*aside*]. I will. [*Calls*] Is Mr. Hudson in, I dunno?

Burl. [*putting his head out of his bedroom*]. Hullo, is that you, Shreedy? No, Mr. Hudson is not in, and he won't take any sparring lesson to-night any way.

Shreedy. Well, I just come to see him about a little matter of business, see? Maybe you might——

Burl. No I might n't. There is not a dollar in the firm, Shreedy, anywhere. Hudson has gone in town. I can't give you a cent, and if you don't get out of here pretty quickly, I may have to borrow a car fare from you. Call again next week. Good evening, and get out. [*Slams door.*]

Shr. Ain't he getting pretty flip? The lippy dude! Maybe he thinks he can put me off that way. Hudson gone in town, ah, rats!

What an old gag. I'll wait round awhile, 'cause I got to have that money to-night. I'll lay for him in this other room, that's what I'll do, and nab him when he comes in. [*Helps himself to two or three cigars and goes into Hudson's bed-room.*]

[*A soft knock on door, then enter Mrs. and Miss Hudson.*]

Mrs. Hudson.   Well, this is strange, I should think Steve would have taken more care to meet us here.

Miss Hudson.   Perhaps he has just gone out for a minute.

Mrs. H.   He ought to have been on the look-out for the carriage, and not compelled us to come up here after waiting twenty minutes at the door.

Miss. H.   He may not have received your telegram.

Mrs. H.   And has gone in town to meet us there? Good gracious! I hope not. Well, we will wait a little while and see. But it is rather awkward for two ladies to be visiting a college room in the evening in this way, even if I am the mother of the occupant.

Miss H. I think it is lots of fun. What a jolly room he has. I wish I were a boy.

Mrs. H. Under the present circumstances, my dear, I wish so too. He *has* arranged his room pretty well for a man.

Miss H. Now, let us look at all his things. We will begin with the mantel-piece.

[*They both turn toward mantel, backs to room.*]

[*Enter Burleigh from his bedroom in evening trousers, no coat or waistcoat, and four or five white cravats in his hand. Without seeing the visitors, he crosses the room to the looking-glass, which hangs on the wall opposite the fireplace, where the visitors are standing.*]

Burl. [*to himself*]. Now for the great agony. Oh, life is very short for this sort of thing. If Steve's family could only see me tying my cravat, they would realize what devotion— [*Suddenly sees women in the glass and starts.*] Good Lord! [*Turns head slowly and looks at Mrs. and Miss H. whose backs are still turned.*] Oh, what in Heaven's name shall I do? I can't get back to my room. Ha! the screen! [*Dives behind a tall screen near the glass.*]

Miss H. Look at all these pipes! And what a horrid smell of tobacco!

Mrs. H. I see that Steve's chum, Mr. Burleigh, smokes. ·

Burl. [*aside over screen*]. And Jack Randolph just made the horrid smell with one of Steve's weeds.

Miss H. [*finding on the mantel-piece a champagne bottle marked "ætat* 21 "]. Oh, look at this!

Burl. [*aside over screen*]. Now she has got hold of the memento of Steve's birthday. What next?

Mrs. H. [*putting on glasses and taking bottle*]. Hm! I suppose that Mr. Burleigh also drinks. I hope my son does all in his power to restrain his comrade.

Miss H. I am so glad we are going to see the great Ned Burleigh at last. Steve says he is so interesting—such a *funny* old bird.

Burl. [*aside*]. Damn him!

Mrs. H. I wonder where they are. One of them must be around, for they would not both go away, and leave their light burning. We cannot wait much longer.

[*Enter Hudson, hurriedly.*]

Hud. Forgot my gloves, of course, and had to come back. Hullo, mother! why, how did you two get here?

Mrs. H. Did n't you get my telegram?

Hud. Telegram? No, I suppose the boy will leave it, on his way to breakfast, in the morning.

Mrs. H. We had to come out to Cambridge to a dinner at Prof. Fullaloves, and thought we would stop on the way back with the carriage, and take you boys into the Assembly. I telegraphed you this afternoon.

Hud. Well, it is lucky I came back. Have you been here long? Have you seen Ned Burleigh?

Miss H. Your chum? No.

Hud. That is good. He must have started in. If you had dropped in on Ned all alone here, he would have had twenty Dutch fits.

Miss H. Now, Steve, before we go, you must show us all your things. [*Picking up photographs from mantel-piece*] Why, who are these?

Hud. Those, er—oh—ah—those—yes. Those

are some of my chum's relations. [*Aside*] Ned
will forgive me for the emergency.

Burl. [*aside over screen*].　Well, I 'll be——

Mrs. H.　I thought those were not yours, dear.

Miss H.　They are all in costume, are n't
they.

Hud.　Yes, yes, private theatricals, you know.
The Burleighs are all great on private theatricals.

[*Enter Prof. Shreedy from Hudson's bedroom.*]

Shr. [*aside*].　Begob, I have him now.

[*Aside to Hud.*]　Mr. Hudson !

Hud. [*turning*].　What ! The devil ! Shreedy !
What do you want here ?　[*Takes him down to
front.*]

Shr.　A little matter of business. Look here,
cully, I want dat ten dollars you owe me for
sparrin', dat 's what I want.　Better let me have
it and not make a fuss before de ladies, see ?

Burl. [*aside, over screen*].　Hurray, bind on
Steve.　Serves him right.

Hud.　I have n't ten dollars, Shreedy.　I
have n't a cent.　Now, do clear out, and I 'll see
you some other time about it.

Shr.　Naw, some other time won't do.

Hud.　I can't talk to you now before my

family. It is bad enough to have them see you round here at all.

Shr. Dat 's all right. Tell 'em I 'm your chum. Just watch me do the nobby. [*Smirks and waves his hat at ladies.*]

Hud. [*aside*]. Oh, this is awful!

Mrs. H. Stephen, who is this person?

Hud. [*aside*]. There is no other way out of it. I can explain later [*aloud.*] This, mother, is my dear old chum, Edward Burleigh.

Burl. [*aside over screen*]. By gad!

Mrs. H. Ah, indeed, I am delighted to meet you, sir. I feel that we are old friends, already, Mr. Burleigh. I have heard so much of you.

Shr. Oh, yes, me and Steve is great chums, ain't we, Steve, old boy? [*slaps Hudson on the back.*] [*To Hud.*] Put me on to de young one.

Miss H. [*aside to Mrs. H.*]. Oh, Mamma, he is awful. How could Steve choose such a man to room with!

Mrs. H. Steve always said he was awkward with ladies, you know. Perhaps he will improve on acquaintance.

Shr. [*to Miss H.*]. Pleased to meet you,

ma'am. How is the state of your health? 'T ain't often we see such a daisy out here, is it Steve? [*To Hud.*] Oh, I can say perlite things to a lady. You need n't be afraid, I won't disgrace yer!

Hud. [*aside*]. How long will this last?

Mrs. H. [*to Hud.*]. Well, my son, I must say, your chum seems hardly the retiring, bashful young man you have always represented him to be.

Hud. Oh, he is, he is. That 's—er—that is just what is the matter. His shyness takes this form, you see. He is really awfully embarrassed, and—er—tries to pass it off in this way.

Mrs. H. Curious forms of shyness.

Hud. Yes, very. It will pass off soon, and you will like him better when the ice is broken.

Shr. [*to Miss H.*]. Ain't that a nobby dress you got on!

Mrs. H. I should think the ice was at least badly cracked already.

Hud. [*aside*]. I must get them out of here. [*Aloud.*] Come, do let us start for the Assembly.

Mrs. H. Well, dear, we have an extra seat in the carriage, and if Mr. Burleigh would like to come, we will wait for him to dress. [*To Shreedy*] Won't you come with us, Mr. Burleigh?

Hud. [*breaking in*]. No—no—no! Ned never cares——

Shr. Why, sure. I 'd be tickled to death. I am wid you easy. Let 's go right away.

Miss H. Don't you want to dress?

Shr. What will I dress for? Begob, I can dance just the way I am as well as the next man. Wait till you see me take de flure. Oh, I 'm a dandy on me toes [*illustrates by a few steps*].

Hud. [*aside*]. Oh, this is too much. I shall have to tell the truth.

[*Knock on door.*]

There!! *Come in!*

[*Enter Randolph, still in his ulster, with the umbrella and smoking the cigar.*]

Rand. Well, Ned, how is——. Oh, I beg pardon! [*Starts to back out; Hudson rushes across and seizes him.*]

Hud. Randolph! Thank Heaven! Come here. [*Takes him aside.*] Jack, have you any money with you? As you love me, Jack, let me have it.

Rand. What the deuce is the matter? I have ten dollars in this coat, but I need it.

Hud. Oh, kind Providence has taken care of its own! Let me have it, I tell you. [*Randolph gives him the ten-dollar bill. Hudson rushes to Shreedy.*]

Rand. Here is a nice position. Is Steve crazy?

Hud. [*aside to Shr.*]. Here, you damned blackmailer. Here 's your money. Now get out, and don't let me see you here again.

Shr. Well, I should have enjoyed the party, but I need the money, so I 'll go. [*To the others*] Ladies, I 'm very sorry, but I find I have a sudden engagement, so I can't keep company wid you to de ball to-night. I 'm all broke up about it, but I hope I 'll see you again. Be good to yourselves. Good-by. Good-by, Hudson, ta-ta.

[*Exit Prof. Shreedy.*]

Mrs. H. Why, Steve, what is the matter?

Hud. I will explain to you some other time. Let me present Mr. Randolph, mother, and my sister. Mr. Randolph is one of my best friends. I *owe* him a great deal. Are you going in to the Assembly, Jack?

Rand. [*decidedly embarrassed*]. No, I can't. There is a dress rehearsal at the Pud ; a *dress* rehearsal, you know, and I must go right round to it now. I just came in for a moment. If you will excuse——

Hud. Oh, nonsense ! Stay a little while. Take your coat off.

Rand. [*aside to Hud.*] Shut up, you jackass !

Miss H. [*looking at Randolph's rubber boots*]. Is it raining, Mr. Randolph ?

Rand. [*uneasily*]. No, no, not yet, no, but it looks like rain.

Miss H. Why, the stars were all out beautifully a moment ago.

Rand. Yes—er—they—er—the stars ? [*With a noble effort*] Ah, yes, yes, the stars *were* out, yes. But, er—they—er—they may go in again, you know. [*Aside*] What rot I am talking !

Hud. Well, it is not going to rain in here, anyway. Do take off your ulster and stay a minute.

Rand. Really, Steve, I 'd like to, but that *dress rehearsal*, you know.

Hud. Oh, let the rehearsal wait. We are going in town in a moment, anyway.

Mrs. H. Don't leave us, Mr. Randolph.

Miss H. [*at mantel-piece*]. Steve, of whom is this a picture?

Hud. [*turning*]. Why, that is Jack himself in the last play.

Mrs. H. Oh, do let me see it. [*Goes to fireplace. Hudson, Miss H., and Mrs. H. stand at mantel with backs to room.*]

Burl. [*from over the screen to Randolph*]. For Heaven's sake, Jack, hand up that ulster!

Rand. [*seeing him*]. What in the name— what are you doing there?

Burl. [*in a nervous and irritated undertone*]. Confound it, man, I have n't any clothes on. Give me the ulster, quick!

Rand. Hurray! Up a tree, are you? You 'll talk to her while I am at the rehearsal, will you? I told you that when I met her you would n't be in it.

Burl. Give me the coat, Jack; do, there 's a good fellow.

Rand. I 'll be hanged if I will!

Hud. [*to his mother and sister*]. Here is Ned's room. I expect it is a chaos just at present. [*They move to door of Burleigh's bed-room, backs still to the rest of the room.*]

Burl. Come round here. [*Steps from behind the screen, and pulls Rand. behind.*]

Rand. [*from behind*]. All right, just for a minute. You promise to give it back. [*Burl. comes out from behind screen, with ulster on. Rand's head appears over screen.*]

Burl. I 'll see. [*Walks towards others. Ladies turn.*]

Mrs. H. Pardon me, Mr. Randolph——Oh!

Burl. Allow me to present myself, Mrs. Hudson——

Hud. Ned Burleigh!

Burl. Quite right, *this* time. *I* am Steve's chum.

Mrs. H. Why, Stephen, I don't understand.

Burl. [*to Hud., severely*]. I do.

Mrs. H. Will you explain this?

Burl. Yes, I think you had better.

Hud. [*putting on a bold front*]. Well, you see, mother, it was just a little joke on Ned. Just a little joke, that is all. [*Forces a laugh.*]

Miss H. Then the other was not your chum?

Burl. Most certainly not.

Mrs. H. Well, I don't understand it yet.

However, I am very much relieved to meet the real Mr. Burleigh.

Miss H.   Mother, I think we had better start for the Assembly.

Mrs. H.   Where is Mr. Randolph?

Burl.   Oh, he has just gone out.

Miss H.   He must have left rather abruptly.

Burl.   Yes, Jack Randolph has very queer manners.   You see, he is awfully bashful.

Rand. [*to Burl. over the screen*].   Here, give me back that ulster.

Burl. [*aside to Rand.*].   I 'll be hanged if I will.   Who is in it now, eh?

Hud.   Well, let us be going.

Mrs. H.   Will you come with us, Mr. Burleigh?

Burl.   I will follow you in later.   I will go down with you to the carriage.

Hud.   Well, come along.

Rand. [*over the screen*].   That is a low trick.   [*Reaches for Burl. with handle of umbrella three times; at third attempt screen falls over and Rand. flat on top of it,—in short ballet dress and pink tights.   His moustache, rubber boots, and decidedly masculine arms and legs make an excellent effect with the garb of a première danseuse.   Ladies shriek.*]

Mrs. and⎫
Miss H.⎭ Mr. Randolph!

Steve. Jack!

Rand. [*nervously spreading umbrella in front of his legs*]. I—I *beg* your pardon. Please excuse my—my *déshabillé.* [*To Hud., savagely*] I told you I was going to the dress rehearsal. [*Kicks Burleigh aside*] I 'll get even with you, Ned.

Mrs. H. Well, Steve, this has been an exciting visit. Does a college room often furnish such incidents?

Hud. Well, it 's all the fault of——

Hud.⎫
Burl.⎭ My awful chum!

14

A HARVARD–YALE EPISODE.

"I 'M off for New Haven to-morrow," Rattleton announced as he dropped into Holworthy's room, where several of the "gang" were sitting. "Going to sojourn two days in the Land of Eli."

"You are, eh?" said Burleigh. "Well, you 'll have a rattling good time down there."

"A '*smooth*' time, you mean," corrected Rattleton. "Don't you know how to talk Elic yet?"

"I beg pardon," said Burleigh. "When you get back I suppose you will refer to the Porc as your 'spot,' and if any of us who are not members asks you anything about it you will cut him dead."

"Don't make any breaks down there about queer pins and extraordinary buildings," said Stoughton.

"They *are* funny about those things, are n't

they?" replied Rattleton. "But I have no doubt they can laugh just as much at us about lots of things."

"Of course they can," asserted Holworthy. "*Vide* the Dickey. That institution is quite as absurd as anything they do down there."

"Nonsense, Hol," protested Stoughton; "whoever thinks up here of taking the Dickey seriously,—except, perhaps, a few Sophomores who are fools and snobs enough to be either cocky about getting on it or sore about being left off. And as for awe and reverence, if there is any such feeling at all towards the Dickey, it is confined to less than a tenth of the Freshman class. What Senior ever cares two snaps about it one way or the other?"

"That may be known well enough to us," answered Holworthy, "but what does an out sider think when he sees Harvard men making such asses of themselves, as those do who are running for the Dickey. Don't you suppose it looks pretty childish."

"For instance," asked Hudson, "if he saw a handsome and accomplished gentleman holding a horse and dog-cart—as I did for you—while a low-down mucker goes in to call on the handsome gentleman's best girl—as you did for me ?"

" That was good for you," laughed Holworthy.

" Or if he saw as I did," added Burleigh, " a dignified swell, named Hollis Holworthy, kissing all the babies he met on the street."

" Or a large and portly person," rejoined Hollis, " lying on his back in the public square at Concord, and telling sympathetic citizens that he was pierced by a British musket-ball. And then running in the dead of night from Concord to Lexington, dressed in a continental uniform, banging on the door of every farm-house with the butt of a musket until he brought out the alarmed householder and told him that the regulars were coming."

" Who made me do it ? " retorted Burleigh.

" I acknowledge I had a hand in it," answered Holworthy. " I am confessing, not defending, *De gustibus Sophomoris non est disputandum.* But that is no excuse. At Yale they don't disgrace their college that way at any rate."

" They may have a lot of poppycock about their mysterious societies that seems ridiculous to us," said Rattleton, " but they don't trouble

anybody else with it. Any way, they are good
fellows, and they always give you a royal time
when you visit down there."

"Yes, they do, my child," Burleigh assented
in a serious tone. "Remember that you rep-
resent the dignity of the 'Oldest and Greatest.'
Take care that they do not make a painful ex-
hibition of our boy."

"Ned knows," chuckled Hudson. "No one
has ever been able to find out exactly what
happened to him when he stayed down there
after the ball-game last year. He came back,
looking like the last hours of an ill-spent life,
with a confused story about some Yale beverage
named 'Velvet' and a wonderful loving cup
with no bottom, and a great many handles."

"Hush your idle scandal," said Burleigh.
"Who are you going to stay with, Jack?"

"A first-rate fellow named Sheffield," answered Rattleton.

"What!" exclaimed Hudson, "Joe Sheffield?"

"Yes, do you know him?"

"Wow!" yelled Stoughton. "Does Steve
know him! Mr. Hudson, do you know Mr.
Sheffield?"

"Shut up, Dick," said Hudson ; "you promised not to tell that."

"I never promised· anything of the kind," declared Dick. "I had almost forgotten it, but I am glad I am reminded. All your friends ought to know about it, Steve. I am sure they would be pleased."

"Hold on!" said Hudson, "if that yarn is going to be told, I prefer to tell it myself. There is no sting in a clean breast."

"Go ahead then," said Stoughton. "I'll see that you tell it straight. Tell the truth, the whole truth, and nothing but the truth."

"It was down at Bar Harbor, last summer," Hudson began. "I was spending two weeks with this man, Stoughton, who lives there in summer. Next to his place there was, er— there was—er——"

"A girl," interjected Dick, putting in the spur.

"Yes, there was, and an awfully pretty one, too," declared Hudson, defiantly. "If you will kindly refrain from interrupting, I can do this thing myself. What I was going to say was this : alongside of Dick's place, there was another place, and a most attractive one. There

was a beautiful view from the piazza of this
house——"

" *On* the piazza," corrected Stoughton.

"Who is telling this story?" demanded
Hudson. " Shut up and let me tell it my own
way. I used to go over to look at this view
every day," he continued; " so did this Yale
man, Joe Sheffield. I used to know Joe at St.
Mark's, and liked him very well, but it was
rather a nuisance to see him at that house so
much. Really he overdid it; why, I used to
find him every time I went there. Finally I
made up my mind that the duel was on, and
I 'd see who was the better man. Of course
this was purely in a sporting spirit, you understand; I only felt it my duty to beat Yale, that
was all."

"Careful, careful," murmured Dick, warn-
ingly. "Remember, –the truth, the whole
truth, and nothing but the truth."

"At first I tried sitting him out by fair
means," Hudson went on, paying no attention
to Stoughton's side remark; " but the persistent
bore outsat me every time. He 'd let me set
the pace and do all the talking, and then come
in with a fresh wind on the finish and do me

up. But early in the struggle a powerful ally presented himself, the girl's small brother, Freddy. He asked me one day why Sheffield wore that funny little pin all the time. I have forgotten now which pin it was ; but it was the symbol of some particularly ' smooth ' and secret band of brothers, and of course Sheffield was never without it. I had been yearning to jab him on his pin; but I knew I could n't pretend to be innocent about it, and it would have been a little too rude to deliberately and openly make him uncomfortable. I told Freddy that I thought the pin had something to do with a club at Yale, but I had no idea why Mr. Sheffield always wore it. I suggested that he might ask Mr. Sheffield himself. It was a mean trick, but I could n't resist it. Freddy said he would, and I knew he was just the boy to do it too. Freddy was of an inquiring and tenacious turn of mind, and never dropped a research on any subject until he had found out all there was to be learned,—he was a very fine little fellow.

. " A little while after that, we three were sitting as usual on the piazza, when my young ally came running up ; as soon as he saw us he sang out in his delightful, eager, childish way, 'Oh, Mr. Sheffield, I want you to tell me something.' Sheffield, pleasant as punch, said, 'What is it Freddy?' You ought to have seen him when Freddy said, 'I want to know why you always wear that funny little pin?'

"Sheffield tried to pretend in the weakest way that he did n't hear him. The big sister told Freddy to run away and play; but Freddy was not the lad to be bluffed that way. He laughed in a knowing way and said, 'Ha-ha, *I* know. It 's got something to do with some club at Yale, has n't it? You have got some secret about it, have n't you? But *I'll* find it out. Nell has secrets too, but I always find 'em out.'

"Hereupon his sister told him that if he did n't mind her, and stop making a nuisance of himself, she 'd tell his father and have him punished. He said he was n't making a nuisance of himself and appealed to me. "Mr. Hudson always tells me all about the Harvard clubs, don't you, Mr. Hudson?'

"I assured him that I did n't mind any such questions at all, and told him (Heaven forgive and preserve me!) that if he would come and see me at Cambridge I would make him have a

first-rate time, and show him the clubs to which
I belonged.

"'There,' he said, 'you don't think I 'm a
nuisance either, do you, Mr. Sheffield? Is n't
there a club at Yale called the Skull and Keys?
I know there is, 'cause I once heard Nell say
she wondered how——'

"His sister grabbed him and said 'Stop' so
severely that she managed to choke him off for
a moment. But it had got too hot for Joe.
He suddenly remembered that he had an engagement at three, at the Kebo Valley Club,
and retreated, leaving the Crimson to wave
alone and victorious over the field.

"Then how that girl did go for Freddy! He
went off almost crying. I tried to stand up
for the little man, and remarked how ridiculous
the Yale men were about their societies. She
did n't agree with me very heartily. She said
it was a relief to see some young men take at
least something seriously, and intimated that
she did n't believe Harvard men were ever
serious about anything, or had any reverence
in them. So for half an hour I dilated on our
great merits, and explained what worthy young
men we really are.

" Next day I tried to 'set' Freddy on again, but it was no use ; he had been temporarily sat on. I was lunching at their house, and for a wonder Sheffield was n't there. I asked Freddy whether he had found out about Mr. Sheffield's club yet. He said 'No, and I can't either. Nell told on me, and Popper said he 'd spank me if I troubled older people any more. I did n't trouble anybody, did I, Mr. Hudson ? I said you had told me yourself to ask Mr. Sheffield about his pin, and Nell said you——'

" I never knew what his sister had said about me, because, just at this point, the old gentle-man banged the table and roared, 'You eat your lunch, sir !' and Freddy subsided.

" A day or two after that, we all went on a picnic. Even Dick, the old hermit, came along, for a wonder. I persuaded his family it would n't be polite for him to stay home, as I was his guest."

" Yes," put in Dick, "you were my guest and I was responsible for your behavior. It was n't the etiquette that worried my family, it was the danger of the thing. Besides, I wanted to see you and Joe Sheffield making fools of yourselves. You did it too, both of you. Go ahead. I won't interrupt you again."

" We all piled into those delightful long buckboards with four or five seats, and drove to the foot of one of the mountains. There is only one defect in the architecture of a Mt. Desert buckboard. It holds three on a seat. Sheffield had to shove himself in on the same seat with the pretty neighbor, so I got in on the other side of her. I did most of the talking during the drive."

(At points such as this during the narrative, Hudson would stop and violently puff his cigar, while Stoughton would hug himself gleefully, and show other signs of delight.)

" We carried the lunch up the mountain," Hudson went on, " and ate it, along with the ants and other things, on the summit. After lunch Sheffield managed to drop me, somehow, and I went off for a smoke with Dick. I consulted with Machiavelli Stoughton, as to how I might again cast down the man from Yale. I knew the crafty Dago could help me, if any one could. Dick wished for Freddy, for Dick always knew how to use that interesting child ; but Freddy had been left weeping at home. Dago

Mac' came up to his form, though. He suddenly pointed to a cluster of brilliant wild
flowers. I said, 'Yes, very pretty. What
about 'em.' Then Dick said 'Do you see
that broad rock this side of them?' It was a
smooth slab that reached from the path, about
twenty feet, down to where the flowers grew.
It slanted at a good steep angle, so that a man
could barely walk down it, with rubber-soled
shoes. I did n't get much inspiration out of
the rock. Then Dick showed me a blackberry
vine, or some sort of a bramble, that ran across
the face of the rock a little more than half way
down it. Still I could n't see what he was driving at. He said to come along and he 'd show
me. We went to the basket where the remains
of the lunch had been stowed, and Dick took
what was left of the butter. Then we went
back to the rock and the Dago greased as much
as he could of it, just above the bramble.
'Now,' he said, 'when we start back for the
buckboard, you fall in alongside of Sheffield
and the enchantress. When you get to this
rock, the method is very simple,—you show the
flowers, Eli will do the rest.'

"At last I took in at a glance all the grand

possibilities of the scheme. I remembered that
Joe Sheffield was very particular about his appearance, and was dressed up to the hilt. He
was always sensitive about his clothes. I fell
upon Dick's neck and wept tears of gratitude.
Then we went back to the rest of the party.
Sheffield had had a monopoly the whole afternoon."

"A corner in Paradise?" suggested Burleigh.

"Exactly," said Hudson, "or perhaps Paradise in a corner. They did n't turn up until we
had shouted for ten minutes and the party had
all started down the mountain. I ranged up
alongside of the pair, thereby breaking up the
Paradise trust, and we three brought up the
rear. When we got to the point in the path,
just above the prepared rock, I called attention
to the flowers, with great art. Of course she
said: 'Oh, how perfectly lovely! Oh, I must
have some of those!' and of course away we
both jumped. I let Sheffield get a little ahead
and then went carefully around the rock. He
bounded gallantly down the face of it until he
struck the butter. Then he sat down with a
dull, sickening thud;—but he did n't stop there.
He glided merrily on, over the blackberry vine,

and in among the seductive flowers. He sat still for a minute, and I knew the situation had dawned on him with all its hideous uncertainties. Then he turned himself round, face to the path, and got up carefully and slowly, with a sort of sideways motion. He did n't attempt to pick any flowers. There was a great deal of sympathy expressed above, and inquiries as to whether he was hurt. Meantime I had arrived safely, picked the whole cluster of flowers, and brought them back in triumph. Sheffield followed me up, and when we moved on, he dropped in behind; he acknowledged the path was too narrow for three.

"On arriving at the foot of the mountain, he leaned up against a big tree, while the buckboards were being manned. The poor girl seemed to be very much worried about him; unnecessarily so, I thought. He assured her that he was not in the least hurt, but he stuck to the tree nevertheless. There was a bird's nest up in the tree, and I heard Dick ask Sheffield to climb up and see if there were any eggs in it, to oblige the ladies. I helped the girl into the buckboard and climbed in beside her. After every one else had got aboard, the last seat, with Dick, was good enough for Sheffield. I ran the Paradise industry, without competition, all the way home. There seemed to be a certain hitch in it, however, for she kept wondering whether Sheffield was hurt. The bunch of wild flowers dropped out on the way, and Dick and I both jumped out and chased it; Sheffield did n't even turn around to see what had fallen. I slapped Dick on the back as we were picking up the flowers and said: 'She must have an opinion of his manners.' Great Scott! that was all I knew about it!"

Here Stoughton went through the hugging pantomime for the fourteenth time.

"She did n't seem to be very grateful when I brought those flowers back, and would n't talk much all the way home. She said she was sure Sheffield was hurt, and all on her account. When we arrived she asked him to dinner. He stayed in the buckboard and drove to his hotel to dress. She did n't ask me to dinner, and, by Jove, she left those flowers over which I had taken so much trouble in the buckboard! I was very grateful to the flowers, nevertheless."

"Well, I don't see where the joke on you comes in," said Holworthy, as Hudson paused.

"Neither did I," answered Hudson. "I thought, in fact, that I had been pretty clever about the whole affair, until—until," he went on, gathering force by the repetition, "*until the engagement was announced!* By Jove!" hurling his cigar butt into the fireplace as the recollection grew on him, "that man and that girl had been engaged all summer; for a week I had been playing smart Alec and steady number three, making her hate the sight of me, while the Yale man was undoubtedly all the time laughing in his sleeve at seeing me make a fool of myself."

"Go on," commanded the relentless Stoughton. "Go on, there is an epilogue,—or do you want me to tell it?"

"No, I'll do the whole thing," said Hudson, humbly. "When Dick and I went round to call after the announcement, and congratulate Sheffield, my little friend Freddy came running into the room. 'Oh, Mr. Hudson,' he shouted, 'isn't it fun! Now we know why Nell got so mad about my bothering Joe. Joe's very nice, but really I would rather have had you, and I told her so.'"

"That wasn't all he said," remarked Dick,

" but I 'll let you off the rest.   I 'll hold it over you for future occasions."

When Rattleton returned from New Haven a few days later, he announced at the table that his friend Sheffield was coming up for Class Day, with his *fiancée*.   He had sent a special message to Hudson to say that they were going to bring Freddy, because Freddy was crazy to see Harvard, and Hudson had promised to show him all over college and take him into all the clubs.

" Whew ! " whistled Hudson ; " d—— that horrid little boy."

THE DAYS OF RECKONING.

JUNE, June, beautiful, glowing, fascinating June, no doubt thou art tired of hearing thy charms sung by lovers more eloquent than I, but forgive this outburst from one who has known thee in the shades of Cambridge. Never art thou more seductive than where the old walls and stately elm trees trace their cool outlines on the turf of the Yard, where the earnest, eager students, prone on the greensward, blow upon blades of grass between their thumbs, and bet on sparrow fights and caterpillar races. The tennis-courts are alive ; there are ball games on Holmes' Field, and the river winding through the green-flowing meadow (the tide being high and the mud covered) is dotted with swift-gliding shells. In the long-fading twilight the bright-beflannelled and straw-behatted groups sit upon the fences, and lounge about the streets, trying to screw up enough energy to disperse to their rooms, and study for the—FINALS.

Ah, June, that is the one worm i' the bud of thy beauty! It is hard, indeed, to eschew the racquet and the oar; to go over to the Library at an early hour and hunt up Story on the *Constitution*, or Dana's *Wheaton*, or Ruskin's *Stones;* to find it seized, and promised to five other men before yourself; to seek a retired alcove less hot than the rest of the drowsy place, and there, taking off your coat, to doze over a volume until four o'clock, when the reserved books may be taken out; then to carry a huge book over to your room, and with an awakening cigar, grind until dinner-time; to go at it again in the evening when the scent of early summer drifts through the open window, together with the singing and laughter of some inconsiderate jackass who has finished his examinations, or does not care whether he gets through them or not. Hard is all this, but still, oh, June, I would woo thee again in those shades even in that wise; for, perchance, I might finish my examinations early and then would I enjoy life to its fullest, and make it miserable for my less fortunate friends. I would join with those who had also finished their work, and we would have a grand reaction. We would urge the others to join us on the river and the tennis-courts; we would sing in the Yard of evenings, and the free would put their heads out of window and cry " More ! More !! " while the still grinding slaves would cry " Shut up ! " and other things that I should grieve to hear and will not state; and if haply we sat upon the steps of Matthews or of Holworthy, or any where within range, these same scurvy slaves would throw pitchers of water and other things, even eggs kept for the purpose, until we untrammelled souls betook ourselves elsewhere. Then would we go to the "pop" concert, or the Howard Athenæum, or other abode of intellectual rest ; and after that we would sup with great mirth. We would found a recuperating club for weary minds, and as each friend threw off the yoke and joined us, we would receive him with becoming ceremonies. Oh ! the last week before Class Day is well worth the pains of the other three.

" What is so rare as a day in June ! " carolled Hudson joyfully, as he danced into his room and thumped Burleigh on the back.

" One in February," growled that portly gentleman, " there are two less of 'em in the year. Now look here ; if you are going to kick up a row because you are all through, just get out of here, and make your ill-timed noise somewhere else."

"Don't be so sour. Hullo, Lazy Jack; these be hard times for you, old Butterfly. How many more have you got?"

"Five," sighed Jack. "Pol. Econ. 23, Fine Arts, Freshman English, and two entrance conditions."

"Great Scott! The way of the transgressor *is* hard."

"Clear out of here," commanded Burleigh. I am coaching this man Rattleton, and I don't want any interruption in my private tutoring. Get out," and Ned hove a dictionary at his exuberant room-mate.

"Oh, if you are laboring with Jack, I won't interfere with the good work of the Rattleton Rescue Mission," said Hudson, dodging the dictionary and taking himself off to irritate some one else.

Ned Burleigh was never in such a mood about his own examinations. He was one of the few men for whom those trials had no terrors. None of his friends could tell exactly when he did work for an examination; it might have been at 4 A.M. on the same morning after a supper ; it might have been on the train during an inter-exam. excursion to Newport, or on a cat-boat cruise in the harbor. Yet he had never failed. He used to say that to know too much about a course made the examinations mere drudgery, but that when there was an uncertainty, then there was some sport in the struggle, some ex-citement as to whether you could throw the paper or the paper would throw you. That was all very well for him, who generally " ragged a B." and never got " flunked," but it was a dangerous attempt for most men to follow his example.

This year, however, Ned was devoting him-self to Jack Rattleton. It was a serious case with Jack, for he had any number of conditions to work off, so many, in fact, that every one was rather astonished at his attempt to retrieve his degree, and at the unwonted, desperate efforts of Lazy Jack. It was a forlorn hope, and the betting was heavily against him. Under any circumstances Ned Burleigh would have done all he could to help poor Jack pull through, but, added to his unselfish interest in his friend, were pride in his pupil and the fact that he had taken

some of the long odds against him. Nor could
Jack have found a better coach in the most high-
priced tutor in Cambridge. With a thorough
knowledge of the courses he had taken, Ned
combined a knowledge of the presiding minds
in those courses, and, moreover, he understood
perfectly the science of passing an examination.

"Now, Jack," he said, "you know the important points and main definitions in that
course pretty well. Just remember that all that
is good is Greek, and all that is Greek is good,
and no modern work from the Brooklyn
Bridge to a beer mug is worthy of aught save
the abhorrence of cultivated men. If the
exam. is in Sever, you might throw in an allu-
sion to the draughts and foul air in that modern pile of bricks. Now how about Pol. Econ.
23? Let's see, does Jowler give that still?
Well, you are morally certain to have a question
on the Tariff of '46—that is his pet. Be certain that the country has never been more pros-
perous than under that tariff. Of course, there
was the discovery of gold and other causes of
prosperity at the same time, but unless you
know all about them, and can explain them
away, don't touch on them at all. Jowler is a

free trader, bear that in mind. I will do him
the justice to say that he would be delighted if
you knew enough about the course and were
clever enough to make any strong points for
protection ; but you are not, so don't try it.
Stick to plain, first principles, and show that
the country is going to the devil."

"Gad, Ned," said Rattleton, shaking his
head in mournful admiration, "it is a great
thing to have learned so much. I have wasted
my advantages awfully."

"Constant application, my son," quoth Burleigh, (who for three years had been on the
ragged edge of probation, and had been saved
only by his high marks), "strict attendance on
lectures, and careful attention to the great men
under whom it is our privilege to sit. Even if
you never go near the library, you can learn
much in the lecture-room. Now I must leave
you ; I am going to a seminar over in College
House."

"All right, I have got to leave, too," said
Jack, looking at his watch. "There is a grinding bee in entrance Greek, in Jim de Laye's
room—lot of foolish virgins like myself, who
have put off the job until Senior year, and are

doing their school work now. By the way, I promised to collar a mucker to drive the horse."

"Get my friend, Mr. James Casey; very intelligent young man; understands the job thoroughly. You will undoubtedly find him playing duck-on-a-rock in a vacant lot back of Holyoke, or badgering the Dago fruit-man on the corner. If you don't find him, drop a package of cigarettes somewhere, and watch it; you will catch a mucker right away."

"A better way than that," said Jack, "is to chain Blathers to the iron railing of the Pudding, and stand behind the door. In five minutes all the best talent in muckerdom will be there with tin-cans and stones."

Jack had no need, however, to expose his faithful hound. He found a covey of muckers, in the vacant lot before mentioned, and on demanding whether any of them could read, was at once besieged with volunteers to "drive the pony." "Chimmie" Casey was among them, and Jack secured his services. "Chimmie" had been at school to some advantage, for he could read Bohn's translations with great fluency (which is the English of "driving the pony "), and made many a half dollar by his learning.

Jack took him round to De Laye's room, where eight or ten men were already assembled, with books, pipes, and siphons of seltzer, ready for the services. The mucker was put in the middle of the room with the "trot"; the students sat around him and followed the translation in their Greek texts. The following is a short specimen of Prof. Casey's flowing delivery of the *Iliad*:

" Den puttin' on deir shinin' mail, dey moved apart from de great crowd of admirin' Trojans and well-greased Greeks. Den Jones spake——"

"What!"

"I can't say dese hard names. Mr. Burleigh told me to call 'em all Jones when I got stuck."

" All right, go ahead."

" Jones spake wid words of hate. 'Dog-eyed son of—son of—' Gosh! dat 's a hard name to call a feller."

" Let it go at Jones."

" 'Dog-eyed son of Jones [I must learn dat], now shalt dou meet dy doom. To him Jones, de god-like son o' Jones—' say, how did dese fellers all have different names from der faders?"

" Never mind ; go on with the trot."

" ' T 'ink not to turn my heart to water wid your vauntin' words ' [always jawin' before dey fight].

" He spake and t'rew his mighty spear and struck full in de midst of Jones' buckler round. It pierced eight folds of tough bull-hide and t'rough de brazen breastplate and cut de linen vest beneat' [dat Jones was a daisy]. Den Jones, poisin' his mighty spear, prayed to Jove : ' Oh, fader Jove, wreak now meet punishment on dis offender; send him to de shades by my arm,'—say, what 's he always stoppin' to talk to dat feller for in de middle of a scrap ? "

" Shut up and go on ! "

" He trew his spear in turn, but de point fell harmless. Den again he cried aloud : ' Oh, fader Jove, dou art de most unkind'—was Jove de referee ? "

" Look here, Jamesey, if you don't stop talking we 'll dock your pay."

" Den sure de light had sped from Jones' eyes, but mudder Venus, when she saw her son hard-pressed, flew to his side. From de field she bore him far from Jones' wrat', wrapped in a hollow cloud [de h— she did! Dat's de silliest fight ever I hear on.]"

At the end of the "grinding bee" young Mr. Casey was dismissed with coins, a cigarette, and advice to restrict his annotations in future lectures.

Rattleton struggled along in his new mode of life for a week or two longer, until his last examination a few days before Class Day. Ned had sent him to bed early on the night before. At breakfast, and on the way over to University, Nestor gave his final advice.

"Look your paper over carefully before you begin to write. Write only on those questions that you can answer, and write a lot on them, so that you apparently have no time for the others. Don't try to bluff on the questions that you don't know; some men can do it, but don't you try it. It rarely goes down with Jowler. Take the whole three hours, and don't go out early, even if you have written all you know. Now, good luck to you, old man; go in and win. I'll see you at lunch."

The paper was very easy. Dick Stoughton had the same course, and finished his answers early. While waiting a decent time for appearance sake, before going out, he executed a characteristic stroke. Brown, the proctor, was a man who prided himself on his sharpness and yearned for opportunities to show it. He was taking a post-graduate course, and had been in the University only one year. He had a custom of walking stealthily about the room, and, in the most offensive manner, peering over men's shoulders while they wrote. On one of these hunts he sat down on the corner of Stoughton's desk and looked over the shoulder of the man in front. Machiavelli Stoughton hastily wrote out, on the back of the examination paper, the gist of half the answers. This paper he pinned on the back of the proctor's coat with the legend "Read him and pass him along." Brown then continued on his tour of inspection, to the edification of all and the salvation of many.

Several other men came out early also. They gathered on the steps of University, and compared notes on the paper. The chief topic of conversation, however, was Rattleton.

"I am afraid the jig is up with poor Jack Rat," said one man. "He is stuck."

"Yes, I saw him biting his pencil and tearing his hair," corroborated another.

" He looked gloomy as a funeral," said Dick ;
"besides that paper was so easy that, if he
knew anything about the course, he ought to
have finished by this time."

" He will lose his degree surely unless he gets
a squint at Brown's back," said Gray. " Can't
anything more be done for him ? Set your
crafty brains at work, Dago Dick."

" Of course, nothing can be done," said
another man. " How are we going to com-
municate with him from out here ? We might
get him in an awful scrape "

" Hold on, I 've got it ! " cried Stoughton,
and dashed off across the Yard.

Half an hour later a man hurriedly entered
the drowsy examination room in University,
and went up to the proctor with a telegram.
Brown looked at the address and took it over
to Rattleton. Jack was now slumped down in
his seat gazing blankly at a fly in his inkstand,
probably wishing to change places with the fly.
The proctor handed him the telegram and stood
near him. Jack opened the envelope, then
started and smiled a little as he read the message. He looked up suddenly and caught the
proctor trying to read the telegram.

"No bad news I hope, Mr. Rattleton," said the latter, looking at him narrowly.

"Oh, no," answered Jack, "best of news." He closed his blue book with a slam and returned the proctor's gaze squarely.

"Ahem!" coughed that officer of the Court. "I presume, of course, Mr. Rattleton, that your message is in no way connected with this examination?"

"I beg your pardon, Mr. Brown," replied Jack in his deliberate drawl, "you do not presume anything of the kind. If you did, you would have better manners than to be so inquisitive about it;—at least I will give you credit for such. As a matter of fact this telegram contains no information on the paper."

"I must insist upon seeing it, sir," exclaimed the red and astounded proctor.

Jack rose to his feet. "You heard what I said," he remarked quietly. "I am not in the habit of being doubted."

He walked up to the desk at the end of the room, and put his blue book on the pile of others. "You notice, Mr. Brown, that I have not written a word since receiving this message. I do not know who sent it, nor anything about it. Here it is if you would like to read it." He threw the telegram on the desk and stalked out of the room.

The group of men on the steps outside crowded around him with eager inquiries.

" I don't know," said Jack, " but I guess I got through. I had written most of the answers half an hour ago, but, of course, I was not fool enough to go out early, and have the proctor mark the time on my blue book. That is all very well for you fellows who are sure of your answers and have good reputations, but I need to exhibit the full three hours of careful thought. I should have stayed to the end if I had n't had a tiff with Brown, the proctor, about a telegram."

" What ! " cried the others. " Dick Stoughton's telegram ? What happened ? "

" Nothing much ; Brown has it."

" Nothing much ! You are a ruined man ! Did n't you see that telegram was a brilliant idea of Dago Mac's. It had all the answers in it ; did n't it, Dick ? "

Jack looked at Dick, and grinned.

" Oh, no," said that crafty genius, "that is only what you fellows thought. I was n't fool
16

enough to write anything of the kind, when that Argus Brown was proctor."

"If he is small enough to look at that telegram after I gave it to him," said Jack, "what he read was this: 'Get into a row with Brown about this telegram. He is a cad, and will probably accuse you of lying. Old Jowler hates that sort of thing, and has no love for the Brown type of proctor. If he hears of the row, he will count it up in your favor.'"

CLASS DAY.

THE conflict of evidence in the case renders it difficult to decide whether Class Day is the gayest or the saddest of the college year. Certain graduates, being duly sworn, depose that it was the happiest day of their whole lives ; an equal number—no, the Court will presume the better—a somewhat smaller number, refuses to testify a: ¹l, until kind Time has obliterated, or, at any ···e, mitigated, important facts in the case ; until, indeed, the memory of man goeth not, or goeth gently, to the harsh Contrary. Most of the Seniors bear witness as here followeth. Were too busy to notice their impressions distinctly ; remember being blue at intervals, decidedly so in the evening. Think they felt jolly on the way to Saunders' Theatre behind the band ; know they felt gloomy in Saunders'. Were worried at their own spreads ; believe the strawberries gave out ; had a very fair time at the other fellows' spreads. Got badly banged around the Tree ; can swear they got more flowers off it than anybody else. Took good care of their families to the best of their knowledge and belief; took their mothers up to their rooms, when affected by the heat ; did not see their sisters ; saw very little of any other sisters. Enjoyed the singing of the Glee Club until it came to " College Days are Over " and " Fair Harvard " ; began to feel a little out of sorts then, and grew more so after everybody had gone. Continued in same frame of mind until the wind-up at the club. How they felt after that some deponents say not, others testify to being still more depressed, and going to bed in decided gloom. On the whole, think the day was a sad one.

On the other hand, the testimony of the Juniors and under-classmen is overwhelmingly on the side of joy. So is that of the rank and file of the army of occupation. The generals, officers of the day, and provost-marshals of that army testify that it is a day of hard work and wearing responsibility. For on that day the largest stronghold of Trouserdom capitulates unconditionally, and from bastion to casemate is swept by the skirts of the invading battalions.

Bright dresses everywhere dot the grass, and float over floors that for twelve months have known only the tread of the trousered boot. Some of the clubs even are surrendered, and only here and there is kept a hiding-place, to which the overpowered defenders may flee to rally on a cigar, or change their wilted armor. The garrison is enslaved almost to a man, each one being attached to the train of some conqueror. During the day the victors are content with such triumph, and show some clemency while their officers hold them in check; but when the shades of evening begin to fall, and the provost-marshals have grown tired, then the slavery is turned into a massacre. Scenes of carnage are everywhere, and the helpless captives are put to the fan without mercy. Some are merely tortured a little, others slaughtered outright, and at the end of the evening many a scalp goes forth dangling from a slender waist. On the other hand, however, it is a solace to reflect that some of the invaders are themselves captured, and paroled for life.

Dick Stoughton had declared that there was to be no tomfoolery for him. His people had gone abroad, and he would therefore incur no

filial liabilities. He rarely went anywhere in
society, and had no civilities to repay. He
thanked Providence that "not one mother's
daughter of 'em had any mortgage" on him.
The only people he invited lived in the far
West, and would n't come. It is often said
that a man never enjoys his own Class Day; he
would see about that. He called for volunteers in the good work. None of Ned Burleigh's relatives were coming East, so he agreed
to stand on Dick's right hand and keep the
strike with him. Randolph was also family-
free and promised to join in the stand for
liberty. These three organized as the Protective Brotherhood of Amalgamated Seniors.

The objects of the Brotherhood were declared
to be lunch, liberty, and the pursuit of happi-
ness. The first rule was to assist each other in
obtaining nourishment and irrigation at the
crowded "spreads." They were to do com-
missariat duty for no one. The second principle was to stand by each other through all the
perils of the day; if any brother should be
captured the others were to rescue him at once,
—three men could resist better than one. They
also arranged a plan of co-operation and mutual

relief, by which any member could talk to any
one he chose without fear of bondage. The
strategic moves were as follows. If one of the
three saw some one to whom he wanted to
talk, he was to notify the others, who would
stand at his back while he opened fire. A time
limit of five minutes was to be allowed him.
Brother Stoughton wanted to cut this down to
two minutes, and Brother Randolph desired
ten. The altercation roused suspicions in
Brother Stoughton's mind, and insinuations on
his part against Brother Randolph's sincerity;
but Brother Burleigh smoothed over the incipient breach and compromised on five minutes.
At the end of five minutes the fire was to be
slackened, and half of the reserves called up
by saying: " May I present my friend," etc.
One of the fresh supports should then wheel to
the front, and while he engaged the enemy,
the other two should go off and find a non-
union man,—a happy, irresponsible Junior, if
possible, one of those important, conceited
Juniors, who wear little silver ushers' pins, and
think they are running the whole thing and
having a glorious time. The two brethren
were to tell this Junior that a very charming

girl had asked particularly to have him presented. Then they should take him up to
where their companion was holding his ground,
throw the Junior into the action, and under cover
of this diversion the three would retreat and
leave him to his fate, pleasant or otherwise, as
the case might be.

Hudson thought the plan an excellent one,
but was precluded from joining by family cares.
Holworthy said " nonsense," and also expected
to be busy all day. Gray declared it was all
out of keeping with the spirit of the day, and
indignantly refused to have anything to do
with it; whereupon the Amalgamated Brethren
called him " scab," and threatened to shadow
him during the evening. Jack Rattleton did
not show much interest on either side, and
indeed was not sure that he would stay up for
Class Day at all. There was something the
matter with Jack, probably the effects of his
abnormal efforts during the examinations.

It rains on Class Day every fifth year, and as
this was only the third, the weather was all
right on the great morning. The vanguard of
the invaders was first met in Saunders' Theatre,
and there held in check and severely handled

for an hour and a half. That was the last resistance offered, however; after that the bright,
victorious masses swarmed everywhere, and reinforcements kept pouring in over the bridge.
The Protective Brotherhood formed square immediately, and bravely cut its way through the
opening spread at the Hemenway Gymnasium.
It moved on the other spreads with equal
success. There was a little friction early in the
day betwixt Brothers Stoughton and Randolph,
because the latter led into action with unneces-
sary frequency and boldness. He wanted to
talk to some one every fifteen minetes, and the
supporting tactics had to be put in operation
too often to suit Dick. Furthermore, Randolph
frequently ran over the time limit.

In the struggle round the Tree, the "gang"
organized itself with great effect. Little Gray
was mounted on Burleigh's shoulders, and with
the others guarding him, tore down flowers
enough for all his supporters. After the Tree,
the Brotherhood prudently united again, and
towards evening went cautiously to the Beck
Hall spread. They had hardly got on the
grounds before Randolph in an undertone
ejaculated the omnisignificant, "By Jove!"

" Are you going in again ? " demanded
Stoughton, impatiently. " You 'll tire us out.
We shall do this thing once too often, the
first thing you know, and one of us will get
stuck."

" You fellows need n't bother about relieving
me this time," answered Randolph, graciously,
and off he went. He was not seen again during
the evening.

" That is what I call rank desertion," exclaimed Dick, in disgust. " I have been afraid
all along he 'd do that. The beggar uses us all
day until *she* turns up, then we can shift for
ourselves.

" Treason, treason ! " cried Burleigh, " let 's
follow him up and make it pleasant for him."

" No," growled Dick, " let these squires of
dames run their heads into the yoke if they
want to. Come on, old man, you and I will
stand by each other, anyway, and live and die
free men. Let 's strike the grub; that Tree
shindy has made me ravenous."

But the " grub " was hard to " strike." Pale
famine threatened over the lawn of Beck Hall.
There was a surging mass around the table in
the tent, and as fast as a dish was brought in

(which was not very fast) it was snapped up by the foragers with cries of " For a lady, for a lady." There was little hope for a free patriot guerilla among these enthralled commissaries of the conquerors.

" Look here," said Dick, " I notice the dishes are brought out of that door. The thing for us to do is to trace these waiters up to their source."

They followed this Stoughtonian idea, and worked up stream against the waiters, until they arrived at the fountain of supply in the cellar of the Hall. The springs were very nearly exhausted, but there was enough salad to load two plates. A demijohn contained one glass-full of claret punch. For this they matched, and Dick won it. Then the explorers returned upstairs, with their brilliantly won booty. Just as they were emerging on the lawn, Dick ahead with his plate in one hand and the glass in the other, they heard an exclamation of " Why, *there's* Mr. Stoughton! " A huge frigate was bearing right down upon them, with all sail set, and four light craft in tow !

Dick's knees shook together, and with a look of astonished horror, he groaned, " Good Lord ! How did they ever get here ?"

" Quick ! " said Burleigh ; " give me the punch. For Heaven's sake save that. You 've got to take your hat off. Hang it, man, where are your manners ? "

In his confusion Dick handed his glass to Ned, and bowed. The next minute the enemy was upon him.

" Oh, Mr. Stoughton, I 'm so glad we 've found you. You must be surprised to see us, are n't you ? So good of you to ask us. I did n't expect to get here, but the girls insisted that they could not miss your Class Day. So we 've come all the way from Omaha. Think of that ! You are the only friend we 've met. Oh ! where *did* you get all that salad ? "

" Ah—er—delighted,—er—so glad you could come," murmured Dick. " Brought the whole family too—this is awfully jolly. By-the-way, let me present my friend, Mr. Burleigh."

Dick turned round for his supporter. Edward was gone ; so was the punch.

Ned Burleigh fled round a corner seeking a secluded nook that he had marked down for emergencies. His intentions were perfectly loyal ; he meant to return and succor his ally after he had safely disposed of the food and

liquid. But he had not gone a dozen steps before he encountered Steve Hudson with a weary
look in his eye. That organ lit up when it fell
on the stout chum and his burden.

"Oh, Ned! where did you get it? Give it to
me."

"There may be a little more where this came
from," answered Ned, sweetly.

"Give it to me, Ned. I want it for my mother.
My whole family is starving on my hands."

"Hum," said Burleigh, suspiciously. "I
think I will take it to her myself. I know this
'for a lady' dodge. If your statement is true,
I want the credit of the sacrifice."

"Good," exclaimed Hudson, the weary look
passing away entirely. "Come along. My
sister has been disappointed at not seeing you
all day."

The sister's alleged disappointment was not
relieved, for she was not with the family at all.
Two or three aunts and a pig-tailed cousin were.
While Burleigh was yielding up his hard-earned
spoils with a hollow, a very hollow grace, and
receiving thanks, Steve Hudson disappeared,
saying he would be back in a moment.

The pale, beseeching face of Dick, languish-

ing among five women, rose before Ned's vision;
but this was no time to think of his comrade;—
he had to forage ice-cream for the aunts. Then
he had to get some water; then he had to look
for the escaped daughter, an unsuccessful quest.
("It's too bad to trouble you this way, Mr.
Burleigh"); then he had to round up two
small boys. ("The boys have no business
here, I know, but they begged so hard to
come"); then he had to take the pig-tail
round the Yard; then more water ("Oh, if
you *could* get some Apollinaris"); Apollinaris;
then he had to order the carriage (" Where *can*
Steve be? We can't go away without saying
good-by to the boy, and telling him what a
good time we have had "); then he had to put
off the carriage; etc, etc, etc. And thus fell
the last of the Amalgamated Seniors!

.   .   .   .

The carriages were beginning to leave.
Ernest Gray got his family off among the first,
and then went on a search.

He looked everywhere, as far as the outlying
spread at the Agassiz; but unsuccessfully. He
came to the conclusion that Class Day was

about over, and began to think that it was not
so merry as he had always thought it before.
As he strolled back over the Delta, it occurred
to him that he would not cross the old historic
battle-ground often again—if at all. Memorial
Hall was brightly illuminated. The light shone
through the stained-glass windows, and showed
the array of those who had done their duty.
The window of '61 caught his eye most plainly.
On the one half was a student listening to the
trumpet, on the other he was going forth full
armed. Over the Senior's head, the calm face
of the Founder looked through the night into
the West,—into the West, where spread the
nation.

He did not go through the Yard, he walked
slowly along behind it. He heard the sound
of music, and between the buildings caught a
glimpse of the enchanted quadrangle, the last
bright transformation scene before the drop of
the curtain. He wandered on and beneath a
well-known window looked up, perhaps from
force of habit. Then he stopped, for, though
the open window was dark, he thought he saw
a form in it. He went up-stairs and knocked at
the door. "Come in," said Jack Rattleton's

voice. The room was unlit, and Jack was sitting in the window-seat with his dog.

"Hello, old man," said Gray. "I have n't
seen you since the Tree. Have you been up
here by yourself all the evening?"

"Well, you see," drawled Jack. "Blathers
was up here all alone, and I thought I'd sit
with him a little while. I can amuse him better
than I can a girl, you know."

Gray walked over to him, and for a long time
the two men of opposite natures looked silently
out of the window together. Below, they could
see the Japanese lanterns, the white dresses,
and all the gay throng—they *could* see them,
but they did n't. They saw, above the elms,
the belfry of Harvard Hall against the clear
night sky. They saw the familiar outlines of
the dark roofs and spires. Over all, they saw
the tower of Memorial pointing to the stars.
Up from the Yard floated, distinctly, the
measures of the Anthem.

> "Thou then wert our Mother, the nurse of our souls
>   We were moulded to manhood by thee,
> Till freighted with treasures, life friendships and hopes,
>   Thou didst launch us on Destiny's sea."

HOW RIVERS' LUCK TURNED.

I.

"WELL, it does concern me, because I don't want any love-sick invalids in that boat." Thus spake the practical William Bender, Esq., Captain of the H. U. Crew. He had just come into Hollis Holworthy's room and sat down for a few minutes' private conversation with that gentleman. By a simple method of his, he had come to the point of the interview in the opening question, "Look here, Hol, is Charlie Rivers in love?" Holworthy, somewhat startled, had replied that his chum's affairs were not his, and intimated that he could not see how they belonged to Bender either. Hence the above remark.

"I don't want you to think," he continued, "that I am merely inquisitive and impertinent; but you see I am responsible for the condition of the men, and if anything of that sort is going on I ought to know it. Last year I had one

man in the boat who was engaged, and two who
wanted to be, and I never knew anything about
it until after the race.   Jim Lovell, who had
precious little money himself, was engaged, to a
girl without a cent, and all the spring he was
thinking about the price of beef when he ought
to have been watching the man in front of him
and improving his recover.   As for Randal and
Bowers they had no right to be in the boat.
They were all out of condition, and I don't see
now how we won.   Even at New London, just
before the race, those two men were moping
like a pair of sick pointers.   They were off
their feed and so blue that they made every
body else so.   I was scared to death, thought
they were overtrained, and laid them off several
times though they needed all the practice they
could get.   I let them fill themselves up with
Bass, nearly a pint a day.   Nothing did any
good, and I never knew what to make of it
until last summer when the engagements of
both were announced.   Bah! no wonder the
starboard side was weak."

" Well, I have heard you rowing men growl
about almost everything," laughed Holworthy,
"but this is a new complaint.   So Dan Cupid

played the mischief with the Harvard crew, did he? I should n't think the little winged god would make such a heavy passenger in the boat. Think how much harder his victims must pull when their fair ladies' eyes are upon them. Why, it is quite like wearing a silken scarf at a tournament."

"Wearing grandmother's ducks. That is just all they know about such things, the chaps who write novels. No amount of ladies' eyes or wearing apparel ever pulled Sir Launcelot through a mill, if he was n't properly trained for it."

"You have no poetry in your soul, you old monk ; your heart is as hard as your muscles," replied Hollis, smiling. "Wait until you get an arrow yourself, and see what a spirit it will put in you. Why, you will conquer anything."

"That is all nonsense,' declared Bender. "Every man on that crew will pull his best, anyway, don't you be afraid about that ; but his best won't amount to much if he spends all his time worrying about some pink and white girl. I think I know the symptoms of the disease now, and what is more I think Charlie Rivers has it. Thank goodness he sticks to

his beef yet, and seems to pull as strong an oar
as ever; but there is something wrong. He
used to be the jolliest old cock in college, and
bright and quick as a steel trap. Now he
hardly talks at all at the training table, and
when he does make a joke it is usually stupid.
You 're his room-mate and best friend, and you
must know what is up. Of course I don't ask
you to betray any confidence, and if he has
been spilling over to you, you are quite right in
telling me that it is none of my business. But
if you have diagnosed his case for yourself, I
wish you would tell me frankly what you think
about it."

" If Charlie is in love he has never told me
so," Holworthy answered rather evasively. " I
do know, however, that he has had a great
many things to depress him. His father died
last winter, you remember, and of course that
was enough to make him blue. Then he has
very little money, and is uncertain about getting any sort of a good job when he graduates,
and he is worrying over that. He will probably brace up after a while. I hope you won't fire
him off the crew, for it would break his heart."

" Well, you know, Holly, it would break mine

too," said Bender. "Charlie has always played in awfully hard luck, and he certainly deserves another chance to win his oar, and a red one at that; but, of course, I can't keep him in the boat out of personal friendship and admiration, if he is not fit to row. I don't think there is any danger of that yet, however. He is still the prettiest oar I have ever seen, and surely no one could work more conscientiously."

"He is a great deal too conscientious. It would do him good to break training once in a while," asserted Hollis. "You ought to let a man in his condition smoke, anyway."

"I don't' know about that," objected the Tory oarsman. "I hope you will do your best to cheer him up, though ; and, especially, if you find out that any girl has got him on a string, talk him out of it and clear his mind."

"Oh, thou untamed Hercules," replied Holworthy, laughing at this last simple request. "I suppose you think you could snap such a string as you can an oar. When Omphale ties you up in her yarn, you won't find it so easy to break."

"Well, I hope old Rivers is not snarled up in any such tackle," said Bender, as he rose to

go. "After all, though, I believe I would
rather have him in the middle of the boat than
any other man in the University,—even if he
were in love with twenty girls." And with this
acknowledgment in spite of such Mohammedan
possibilities, Billy Bender went off to the river.

As Bender had said, Charles Rivers had been
"playing in hard luck." Though a splendid
oarsman he had never won a race. In his
Freshman year he had been taken out of his
class crew to be a substitute for the University
eight. The next year he rowed No. 4 on the
'Varsity; but Yale won. He filled the same
place all through his Junior year, until a week
before the race, when he sprained his heel and
had to sit in the referee's launch and watch his
comrades get their revenge on the Blue. This
year was his last, and he had begun training,
even with the new men, before Christmas.

Few people realize through what a man must
go who tries for a university crew. Even those
who have been to the rowing colleges cannot
fully appreciate it unless they have themselves
trained with the big crew, or been closely
associated with some man who has done so.
True, it is only to lead a very regular abstemi-

ous life, and to do a good deal of healthful, though hard work. It may seem easy to do this for seven months—perhaps it is so for those superior to the little vices that make life pleasant for us weaker ones. But you, my friend, who like a good dinner and a cigar, and the merry company of your fellow-men, you try it,—particularly if you are living in the midst of men who are enjoying their youth to its utmost. Leave them before ten o'clock and go to bed just as Tom is preparing to make a Welsh rarebit, and Dick is brewing a punch, and Harry has got out his banjo. Gaze day after day on your favorite pipes that look beseechingly at you from the mantel-piece. Run five miles every day, and row ten or fifteen while the coach and coxswain take turns at telling you how utterly useless you are ; then try to study all the evening for an examination. Watch your friends starting off without you on moonlight sleigh rides, and theatre sprees, and yachting and coaching parties. Go to a dinner and refuse everything indigestibly tempting that is put under your nose, look on the wine when it is red and don't drink it, and smell the other men's cigars. For six or seven months out of

the nine of a college year he must do all this
who would be one of the 'Varsity Eight ; and
at the end of the seven months he may be
appointed substitute, or thrown off altogether
for a better man.   No doubt it is quite wrong
to consider such a proper mode of life as a
sacrifice ; nevertheless it is a great one to most
of the young men who go through it, and particularly to such a one as Rivers.   Yet this
sacrifice he had made all through his college
course.

But hard as the training is to a man in the
full flush of health and spirits, it is ten times
harder to one who is troubled and depressed.
When in such a condition the incessant and
monotonous exercise is apt to wear on his
nerves, and make him more despondent.   If
used to tobacco he wofully misses the great
comforter.   So poor Charlie found it, for in
this, his Senior year, one thing happened after
another to grieve and worry him.   In the winter his father died, and Rivers keenly felt the
loss, for his father had been his best friend.
Added to his natural grief was a new feeling of
responsibility, as though left to fight a battle
unsupported, his reserves having been de-

stroyed. On his own account he would not
have been troubled by this, but a young sister
had been left to him—and very little else. He
would have left college at once, but it had been
his father's earnest wish that he should take
his degree, and there was little chance of finding anything to do before Commencement. So
the little sister was quartered with an aunt,
and Rivers came back to Cambridge, and went
to work again with the crew. The training wore
on him more than ever before. He did not
miss the fun that was going on around him,
but, oh! how he did long for his pipe. He
kept grimly on, however, more with the deter-
mination of the man (trivial though the object
may seem) than with the former enthusiasm of
the boy. Holworthy used to do his best in the
evenings to lighten his chum's mood, and never
smoked himself when the latter was with him.

Besides these troubles, Hollis strongly suspected that there was another; he had not
been altogether frank with Bender on the subject. One day some one and her mother came
on to Boston for a fortnight, and Rivers at the
same time became bluer and more restless than
ever. He put all his pipes out of sight, and

would tramp up and down the room, or sit and look into the fire for an hour at a time. Nevertheless he would go into Boston nearly every day, and get back only just in time for crew practice.

When some one and her mother came out to see Cambridge, a luncheon had to be given in the room. There was the usual borrowing of furniture, ruthless clearing up, and upsetting of all established disorder in the room, all of which Holworthy suffered in silence. He watched his patient narrowly all through lunch; but when they went out to see the lions, he no longer had any doubt about the case. For Rivers took Mamma, leaving Hollis to convoy the younger craft.

Before the two weeks were up, Rivers did a very foolish thing. He came to the conclusion that, in any event, hell would be better than purgatory. That was of course illogical, but a man in purgatory is not logical. Furthermore when he makes up his mind to jump out of that middle place, he shuts his eyes and always hopes, with or without reason, that he will not go the wrong way. If he were in a comfortable state and could reason at his ease, he might not

delude himself with unfounded hope. Charlie
Rivers thought he had argued coolly with himself. To the prospect of his responsibilities
and narrow means, he answered that he had
strength, energy, and education, and that his
little sister needed more than money. To the
cold reflection that he had never been shown
the slightest glimpse of anything more than
the dictates of natural gentleness and good
manners, he replied that perhaps it was not
right for a girl to show more until a man told
her that he loved her. At any rate he would
not trust his untutored perceptions to tell
whether she cared anything for him or not;
the only way was to ask her and find out. If
he was afraid to do so he was a coward and did
not deserve her. Then he argued himself into
the idea that it was his duty to tell her squarely
how he stood, and give her the opportunity to
send him away if she so pleased and put a stop
to attentions that might be irksome to her.
This was all very silly and boyish. If he had
known all about such things, as of course do you
and I who read and write about them, he would
have spent that Sunday, on which there was no
rowing, in his room, reading Thackeray, or gone

out with Rattleton and Holworthy in the
former's dog-cart, as he was asked to do. Instead of either of these safe and normal Sab-
bath amusements, he hurried away from his
untasted lunch at the training-table (making
Bender's blood run cold by showing that he
was " off his feed "), spent an hour in dressing,
and then went in to Boston.

That afternoon as Holworthy and Jack
Rattleton were driving through a suburb of
Boston, they saw walking ahead of them a big,
familiar form, towering beside another form of
very different proportions. Rattleton laid the
whip over his horse and went by the couple at
a pace that precluded any sign of recognition.
Holworthy was as much surprised as pleased
at this thoughtful act on Rattleton's part ; and
concluded that he must in some way have
guessed that things were serious with Rivers,
and no subject for teasing. Nor did Jack say
a word about the pair of pedestrians, or hint
that he had recognized Rivers, which reticence
confirmed Holworthy's conclusion. On this
drive Rattleton did not talk a great deal about
anything. He had been quite despondent
lately and unlike himself, probably on account

of the uncertainty of his Commencement, though the dreaded end of Senior year was still a good way off by Jack's ordinary computation. On two evenings within that past week had he been found in his room, "grinding" for that degree, when the examinations were still two months away.

It was dark when they got back to Cambridge, and went up to Holworthy's room to sit until dinner-time. There was a dark mass on the couch, and when they lit the gas they saw Rivers. The young giant was lying on his chest, his great arms over his head and his face in the cushions.

"The old boy is over-trained and tired," whispered Rattleton. "I had better clear out and not waken him," and he left the room.

Had Jack recognized Rivers that afternoon or not? wondered Holworthy. He hoped not. He turned the light out again, not knowing exactly why. Then, after a moment's hesitation, he went up and laid his hand gently on the shoulder of his prostrate room-mate. Let us not turn the gas up again on those two. We will go down-stairs instead with Jack Rattleton.

As he closed the door gently after him Jack

gave a little low whistle. Then he went slowly down-stairs and into the Yard, followed by the dog, Blathers. "Come along, pup," he said to his constant companion; "let's go take a walk." He walked a long way and came back to his club table rather late for dinner.

Holworthy was late, too. As they were smoking with their coffee, the other men having gone, Rattleton asked if Rivers was not getting "stale" from his training.

"I think so, decidedly," answered Hollis. "I have spoken to Bender about it, but he is such a conservative old martinet that he won't break any of the canons of training until he is satisfied that a man is going into a rapid decline. I know a cigar once in a while would do Charlie more good than harm, but I can't make the conscientious beggar steal a smoke without permission from his tyrant. He is blue as indigo."

"Is he troubled about money matters?" asked Rattleton, hesitatingly coming now to what he wanted to find out. "Did n't his father leave him rather hard up? Excuse my asking, but I thought we might help him to find something to do, don't you know."

"That is a great deal of the matter with him,"

answered Holworthy, glad to see the tack on which Jack was steering. "You need n't apologize for asking about it. I wish to thunder we could find him a job. He is worrying all the time about what he is going to do after leaving college."

That night Rattleton wrote a letter to his father, who was president of a big corporation.

From this time on Rivers seemed to brace up in his mental, and consequently in his physical condition. This apparent improvement, however, did not deceive Holworthy, who saw that it was, in a way, unhealthy. Rivers had kept at his rowing and training patiently and doggedly before; but he now threw himself into it heart and soul as a distraction. He dreamed of the coming race night and day. He tried his best to seem cheerful and encourage the other men, and his plucky efforts succeeded very well. Bender was delighted, declared there was nothing like faithful training to keep a man in proper shape, body and mind, unless he was fool enough to fall in love, and concluded that he had suspected Rivers unjustly on that score.

The latter showed every now and then to his chum the intensity, almost fierceness, that lay

under this apparently happy enthusiasm. One
day he said that he must make a success of at
least one thing before leaving college, and if that
race were lost he should feel as though he were
going to fail in everything he undertook all
through life. Then Mentor Holworthy opened
on him with all his batteries. He told him that
he ought to be ashamed to make such a mere
sport the test of his life ; he descanted hotly on
the subject of the athletic fever, and laughed
scornfully at the fancied importance of such
intercollegiate contests.

"I suppose," said he, "that Hancock and
Adams and Emerson and Longfellow and all
the rest of them will sleep more peacefully in
their graves if we beat Yale, and if we get
thrashed no doubt old Dr. Holmes will be sorry
he ever came to Cambridge, and will at once go
down to New Haven to take his entrance examination for the Freshman class there. Have n't
you grown up yet, that you look on these
things as a school boy? These overwrought
struggles can do good in just one way, and you
seem ready now to throw away even that advantage. Every time a thoroughbred gets licked
it does him good. You have seen the men on

our different teams get up after a thrashing and go at it as hard as ever the next year ; you have yourself gone through a splendid school of defeat and disappointment, yet now you talk about lying down for all your lifetime if you lose a boat-race. It is true you cannot row against Yale again, but there is a bigger victory than that to be won. Have you for the first time lost all your heart after a failure? You of all men should not need to be told that a prize is never lost until won. At any rate lay up in reserve for yourself the consolation of having done your best. Charley, Charley, if you throw up the sponge after one knockdown, you are not the man I have always thought you."

Rivers listened to all this, with head bent. When Hollis stopped he raised his face again and said : " I know what you mean, old man, and you are right. I won't lie down like a cur. I 'll pull it through to the finish, anyway. But in the meantime I must do like a man whatever I have taken up."

" Now you are talking like your old self," answered Hollis, " but don't forget that doing your duty like a gentleman is not confined to rowing a boat-race."

18

After this broadside Rivers went on with his rowing in a better spirit than he had shown during that year. Before long he was immensely cheered up also by the promise of a position with a good salary and chance of advancement, that was to be ready for him right after the boat-race. Jack Rattleton, through his father, had succeeded in getting this for him. His absorbing devotion to his rowing fortunately did not prevent him from getting his degree but he lost a *cum laude* and had to " take his A.B. straight," as Burleigh said, "without any green leaves or nutmeg in it."

There was another piece of parchment made out for Commencement Day, that was a surprise to every one. It was marked Johannes Rattleton.

II.

Class Day and Commencement were over, and every one was now bound for New London to attend the post-Commencement carnival that, for the undergraduate at least, really winds up the college year. The crew had gone down to their quarters at Gale's Ferry two weeks before; there had been no Class Day for them. The faithful flocked to the Thames' mouth in squads and divisions, and by all sorts of methods, some in big yachts, some in cat-boats, others on coaches, but most by train at special rates, for the undergraduate is usually not rolling in wealth, particularly at the end of June. The fresh graduate who has just paid his Commencement bills is still less apt to do any coaching or yachting except by invitation.

Dick Stoughton however had a small sloop, and he and his friends had decided that the cruise would not "break" them, and at any rate that they would make it whether it broke them or not. It would be cheaper to live aboard, they argued very plausibly, than to get swindled by New London hotel-keepers. They would refrain from betting on the race; then if Yale won they would be no worse off financially, and if the Crimson went to the front they would not spend twice their winnings on the spot, as they would be sure to do if they bet. This was a highly praiseworthy resolution, and of course the most sensible way of looking at the folly of betting. Burleigh said it was easy enough to look at anything sensibly. They would go, then, on Dick's sloop, and they would not bet a cent. They went on the sloop. The party was made up of Stoughton, Hudson, Randolph, Burleigh, and Gray. Holworthy did not go; he had taken a room in New London at the Pequot House, and went there immediately after Class Day, as he wanted to see all he could of Rivers at the quarters. Strange to say, Jack Rattleton also refused all persuasion to join his friends on the cruise. In vain did Ned Burleigh, with tears in his eyes, assure him that it would be the last and most beautiful "toot" of his college course. Jack advanced several good but utterly insufficient and unnatural reasons for "shaking the gang." Ned exhorted him more in sorrow than in anger.

"What has got into you lately?" he asked anxiously. "That sheepskin seems to have ruined you. I actually believe you have re-formed, or have caught a premature aim in life, or some such fatal disease. You were a great deal better fellow when you were Lazy Jack and did n't amount to a row of pins; John Rattleton, Esq., A.B., is a bore. You strained yourself badly for those letters, and are run down in consequence. Hang it all, Jack, come along, it will do you good."

But Rattleton did not go along. He hung around Cambridge until the day before the race, and then joined Hollis at the Pequot House. Capt. Stoughton's craft had arrived safely, notwithstanding her crew, and was anchored in the river with the rest of the fleet in front of the hotel, when Rattleton got there.

The night before the boat-race at New London is one that bears recollection better than description. The Pequot House is usually the centre of ceremonies. Crowds of men are down from Cambridge, and there are a few of the advance-guard from New Haven, although most of the Yale men come next morning. Lectures and examinations are behind them, the long vacation is ahead ; it is the last spree of the year, the last gathering of the four years for the Seniors,—and full justice is usually done the occasion. Many a grad., too, runs away from his office to the Connecticut town, or comes ashore there from his yacht, to renew his youth on the eve of battle and to shout at the struggle on the morrow.

Of course on that evening the party from Stoughton's boat were ashore, and in the thick of it. Ned Burleigh was master of ceremonies,

and organized a band of "cheerful workers."
Holworthy, however, kept out of it. He was
thinking of eight men up the river, five or six
miles away from all this roystering, and of one
big man in particular, whose whole soul, like
his muscles, was strung up for the next day.
He wondered whether Rivers was getting any
sleep, and the anxiety about his best friend left
him little heart to rollick with the others. He
was surprised to find Rattleton in much the
same mood, for notwithstanding the recent
change in that young gentleman, it seemed
hardly possible that Jack could sulk in his tent
at such a time as this. The two, with the dog
Blathers, walked out together on the piazza.

As they turned a corner of the veranda they
saw sitting in the light of a window two
feminine figures, one of which Holworthy at
once recognized.

"By Jove!" he thought to himself; "has
she come down to see that man kill himself, or
does she really want to see him win?" Then
he growled to Rattleton, "This is a nice place
for a girl on this evening, is n't it?"

Rattleton had stopped short. "Look here,"
he said, "you go warn those Comanches, and

keep them in bounds. I am going to talk to her."

"Why, do you know her?" queried Hollis a little surprised.

"Oh, yes,—slightly,—well enough to speak to. You go along."

Holworthy went to the back of the hotel, and Jack towards the two ladies.

"Why, how do you do, Mr. Rattleton," said the younger one, as he came up and bowed. "Let me present you to my aunt, Mrs. West."

"Are you staying in the hotel?" asked Jack after the opening salutations. Just at this moment he heard, from the direction of the billiard-room, the silvery voice of Mr. Edward Burleigh, leading the cheerful workers in the strains of a hymn. He was greatly relieved when Mrs. West answered, "No, we are staying in one of the cottages, and came over here only for dinner. Ethel, my dear, I think we had better go back now. You will walk over with us, Mr. Rattleton, will you not?"

"With pleasure," answered Rattleton, truthfully. "Do you mind my dog?" On the contrary, they thought Blathers a lovely dog, and all four went over to a quiet cottage at a little

distance from the hotel. The veranda looked
out over the beautiful river and was most inviting. It was apparently not so, however, to
Mrs. West; for as she went up the steps, she
said: "I feel a little chilly, and am going in
doors, Ethel. You may stay out here for a
little while, if you like." Ethel did like and
went over to a pair of chairs. As she passed
through the light of an open door, Jack caught
sight of a bit of blue ribbon pinned on her dress.
He sat down opposite her, and opened the
conversation, by remarking, "You are on the
other side of the fence, I see."

"Oh, yes," she answered. "Don't you know
that I have a cousin on the Yale crew? I am
very proud of him."

"Oh, have you?" said Jack, with an inward
groan. "I did n't know it. Well, I never was
a really clever, polite liar, but I am not such a
transparent one as to say that I hope he will
win."

A little rippling laugh followed this confession. "No, you had better not strain the truth
to that extent. I will forgive you for sticking
to your colors and for being so frank about it."

"It is not only because I am a Harvard man

that I want to see our crew win," Jack went on
with a sort of gulp, "it is also because the
most splendid man I ever knew, and one of
my best friends, is in the boat. He has been
through an awful mill, and deserves to win if
ever a man did."

"Indeed?" came the question, perfectly un-
interestedly. "And who is that?"

"A man named Rivers. Do you happen to
know him?" Rattleton tried to see in the
moonlight whether or not there was any more
color in her cheek; but he could n't. Besides,
he had enough to do in looking after his own
face. He felt cold all over.

"Oh, yes, I know him quite well," she answered, quite carelessly. "Nice fellow."

"He is more than that, he is a hero," declared Jack. "You can hardly form any idea
of what that chap has been through this year,
and the way he has borne it all is splendid. He
has had all sorts of troubles ; his governor died ;
he was blue about his exchequer ; and last, and
worst of all,"—Jack was glad the moonlight was
kind to him also, but looked at his boots, nevertheless,—"I am perfectly certain that he fell in
love with some girl and got a facer."

" A what ? " exclaimed his listener.

" I beg your pardon—a staggering blow in the face, metaphorical, of course. I have got so in the habit of using slang, that I fear I am not fit to talk to a lady. I beg you will forgive me for bringing such prize-ring language to your ears."

" It is very expressive, at least," she said. " And did Mr. Rivers tell you that he had received a facer ? "

" No, no, no," protested Jack, " of course not. I don't *know* it, I only suspected it from his actions and condition. I don't even know, of course, who the girl is. But whoever she may be, she is making a big mistake. She is throwing away the most magnificent fellow in the world. If she does not amount to anything," he went on slowly, " I am glad she does n't take him, for Charley ought not to be wasted on her. But if she is the most beautiful, gentle, sweet woman who ever lived, then, by Jove, such a pair ought to be married. And I am sure she must be just that, or else, you know, Rivers would not have fallen in love with her. Don't you think so ? "

Rattleton's hair was rigid at his boldness and

impertinence, but his hair had nothing to do with his speaking apparatus. His heart was taking charge of that, moving it very slowly and just a little hoarsely.

" Why, what devout hero worship!" said the girl with a smile. " No, I don't think anything of the kind. He might have fallen in love with some one entirely unworthy of him, or, what is more, who did not care for him. No matter how perfect she might be, you would not have her marry if she did not love him, would you?"

" No—o," assented Jack, reluctantly, " but she ought to love him."

" He must, indeed, be all that you paint him, then," she laughed, " but love does not necessarily take to paragons, you know. Why do you admire him so very much?"

" Because I have known him like a brother for four years," answered Jack, earnestly. "Oh, if you knew him as well as I do, you would——you would n't think I was exaggerating."

"What made you think him so desperately in love?"

"Oh, I don't know. I think it is unmistakable," was Jack's weak reply.

"Only those can tell who have themselves been in that condition—they say," came the laughing response.

Jack's finger-nails went into his palms. "No, no," he stammered, "no,—I can tell. Oh, you ought to have seen him," he went on, desperately. "The way he went to work at that rowing after it all, showed his sand. If they lose to-morrow, I believe his plucky old heart will break right in two."

"And is his 'sand,' as you call it, restricted to rowing a boat-race?"

"No, I did n't mean to imply that. He will go on working to win that girl in every way he can, I am sure. I only meant that his conduct about his training, in such a hard time, shows what stuff he has in him."

"Do you think, then, that winning a boat-race is the best way to win a wife? Might not Mr. Rivers find some higher field for his qualities? Is it not a little childish to make an athletic contest the aim of a man's life? Do you think the only pluck worth admiring is that which goes with muscle?'

Jack had heard endless discussions on this subject, and was ready for these questions.

" No," he said in answer to the last one, " I
don't think anything of the kind. Please don't
imagine that at Harvard we are nothing but
gladiator worshippers. We admire a plucky
athlete, it is true, but not because he is strong
or successful, only because of his grit and self-
denial. Of course we want him to put the
Crimson ahead, but we like him none the less
if he fails, provided he has done his best and
done it like a gentleman. We admire the
same qualities just as much when we see them
in any other field than that of athletics, but I
suppose we don't recognize them so easily.
But in that our little world is not so different
from the big one. Now I am going to ask you
some questions. Has any man during the last
seventy years been elected President of these
United States for his greatness, unless he was
a soldier? Has not the general been preferred
time and again to the statesman? Has not
the warrior always been dear to the heart of
the people, while other men, who have hammered away all their lives with longer-winded
pluck and perseverance, must content themselves with secondary honor? The reason of
this must be that when a man does his duty on

the batticfield, his merit is more patent to the
people than in the harder and less showy
struggle of civil life. Are we youngsters, then,
so very much younger than the old and wise
ones who criticise us? Why, you yourself just
now said that you were proud of your cousin
because he was on the Yale crew."

"Oh, no, I did n't say that," laughed the
girl; "I only said that he was on the Yale crew
and I was very proud of him. Why, Mr. Rattleton, what a sharp pleader you are! I had
no idea that your talents lay in that direction."

"By Jove! neither had I," exclaimed the
ingenuous Jack, really wondering and somewhat abashed at his unaccustomed volubility.
"I am only trying, you know, to repeat what I
have heard other fellows say," he confessed,
apologetically. "I suppose I have got it all
mixed up and am talking like a fool, but please
make allowances for me, because I am one, you
know."

"No you are not at all," she said slowly, to
Jack's great relief. "But don't you think that
you rather belittle yourself and your fellows by
being too humble, and comparing yourselves
with people who have not had your advantages?

Ought not educated men, men of the same school that has produced our greatest thinkers and workers, ought they not to discern between the showy and the solid ? Should the manliness of the athlete be any more patent to them than the higher courage of the student ?"

" I suppose not," admitted Jack, resignedly. " That is just what Holworthy always says. I tell him he is a prig, but of course he is right, and so are you. But nevertheless, childish or not, I cannot help admiring such a man as Charlie Rivers for the qualities he has shown. He has been so strong and patient and loyal, —oh ! such a *man*. No, even if it is all wasted as you say, you can never convince me that I ought not to love him for it."

There was silence for a moment, and then came the admission very softly. " No, I don't think I can." Jack's finger-nails went into his palms again.

A moment later she arose and said : " Really I ought not to keep my aunt up any longer. I must say good-night, Mr. Rattleton."

Jack jumped to his feet. " I beg your pardon for staying so late," he said. " The time has gone fast. And–er–by–the–way," he continued, a little awkwardly. "I have done wrong in talking so much about Rivers' trouble. Of course, I really know nothing about it, and it is none of my affair, you know, anyway. Please don't think that I am in the habit of gossiping about other men in this way. I got rather carried away to-night, I am afraid. I beg you won't say anything about it to any one."

"I never make conversation out of such things, Mr. Rattleton," she answered. "You may depend that I shall not repeat it to a soul. And now good-night."

She looked into his eyes with a radiant smile, and held out her hand. Jack took it as if he were afraid of breaking the little thing, and then dropped it quickly. "Good-night," he said, shortly, and went down the steps and over the lawn, followed by Mr. Blathers.

She stood for a moment and watched him putting great stretches of moonlit grass behind his long thin legs, the little dark figure trotting beside him. Then she went in, threw her arms around her aunt's neck, and kissed her.

"Has Mr. Rattleton gone?" asked Mrs. West. "He seems like a nice fellow."

"Yes, and he is one. When I first met him,

I thought him easy enough to understand, and like every other boy; but I can't quite make him out now. At any rate he is a species new to me and an interesting one "; and she ran up-stairs to her room, singing.

Jack Rattleton strode along the river bank and out to the end of the Pequot pier. He stood there for a minute, looking over the river and Sound, then sat down on a bench. That enchantress, the moon, was aided in her fairy work by the riding lights of the dark fleet of yachts at anchor, and by the colored sailing lights of the becalmed late comers drifting in from the Sound. But the lights only hurt his eyes. He had sat there some time when he heard his name spoken.

" Beautiful, is n't it," said Holworthy, behind him.

" Got a weed? " asked Jack.

" Yes."

" Give it to me." He bit off the end of the cigar nervously, and lit it with thick puffs. " Gad! " he muttered, I 'm glad I 'm not training for the crew. How did he ever stand it! But Charlie Rivers is a very different breed of cats from me."

19

Holworthy looked on a moment in silence, and tried to pull an idea out of his moustache.

"What is the matter with you, Jack?" he asked, gently.

"Nothing—only that I am such a poor sort of a thing. No ambition, no backbone, no sand. Just a worthless, dissipated loafer. Let's go lush up with the rest of the crowd,— that is all I'm good for."

"Don't talk like a fool," replied Hollis, by way of comfort.

"A disgrace to the University. Have n't you always told me the same thing?" asked Jack, with a ghastly grin.

"That is no reason why you should think so yourself and get so blue about it. I never thought you would ever take it to heart so. You know I never meant half that I said. I used to lay it on thick in hopes that a little would soak in."

"I wish it had all soaked in long ago," answered Jack, ruefully. "Don't take any of it back, old man; you have n't soured me. Come along, let's go back to the old gang. You are all a very bad lot and don't properly appreciate my faults; even you, you old prig. Come along, Blathers."

He tucked his arm through Holworthy's and they went back to the hotel, Hollis musing much.

Meanwhile, in the billiard-room the good work was going on to Ned Burleigh's deepest gratification. He himself, mounted on the pool-table, was beating time with a broken cue for a choir of sweet singers. They had cheered each member of the crew and the coxswain, declaring in the time-honored measures that each was a jolly good fellow, and intimating the mendacity of any one who might deny the fact. Grateful for his degree, and being in a broad and liberal frame of mind, Burleigh had also proposed each member of the Faculty of Harvard College for similar honors, prefacing each nomination with a few well-chosen remarks.

" And now, dearly beloved brethren," said he, " omitting the next fifty-three stanzas, let us all unite in singing the one hundred and forty-fifth ; and as I look upon your happy, up-turned faces, I cannot help being touched by the spirit of those beautiful lines. All sing! "

The earnest chorus roared, with cheerful zeal, the one hundred and forty-fifth verse, as exhorted.

" **What ho!** " shouted the Lord of Misrule,

" What is yon tall form i' the doorway. Is it
the melancholy Jacques, forsooth ? Or is it our
long-lost wandering Brother Rattleton returning to the fold ? Pull off his coat, somebody,
and look for strawberry-marks. Joy, joy, mark
his old time smile ! Throw him up here. Once
more now, all sing, " For he 's a jolly good
fellow ! "

III.

The day was beautiful and the water perfect,
a most unusual combination for the 'Varsity race,
day. All the steam yachts had gone up the
river, and most of the others towed up also and
anchored along the course near the finish. It
would be waste of time to try to describe the
picture of the great annual event of oardom, a
picture that is done every year in the sumptuous
paints of the press, with the sky and the river
and the yachts and the crowds, and above all
the two colors everywhere. It is painted every
year, but no one can appreciate it who has not
seen the original. It is not for this spectacle,
however, that all these tremendous crowds
gather ; it is to see two long thin yellow streaks,

each surmounted by nine bodies, eight of which swing back and forth in a most monotonous, uninteresting manner. That is all that the race looks like to most of the spectators—then why do they go to see it? Because they know that those sixteen men are going through about the hardest physical strain that men can bear. To the layman there is in tennis and base-ball four times the skill and pretty playing that there is in foot-ball, and in rowing there is none at all. Yet a tennis match excites the least interest of all college sports, base-ball comes next in the rising scale, and both of these combined do not rouse a quarter of the enthusiasm provoked by a foot-ball game. But at the head and front of all athletic contests is rowing—because it hurts the most. Foot-ball, it is true, requires a dashing courage and disregard of breaks and bruises (though " dashing courage " and all that sort of thing never occurs to the struggling youngsters), but there is always the great relief of frequent short rests during the game ; in a four-mile boat-race there is no let-up. The half-back makes his rush and plunge, is slammed on the hard ground and buried under hard muscle, is picked up, rubbed a little, and with the cheers of the crowd in his ears again goes at the line, head first, as hard as ever. But for the oarsman there is only the incessant pull, pull, pull, with the bees in his brain and the growing hole in his stomach, the aching legs and leaden arms, and before him, growing dimmer and dimmer, the bare back that will never stop rising and falling, and that he must follow, it seems, to death. Oh! it does hurt, and that is why the great crowd goes to see it and goes wild. Yes, fair and gentle one, that is just why even you go to the Thames as your predecessor went to the Colosseum. There is this vast difference, however, between you and Octavia—the Roman Vestal looked at hired gladiators, and prisoners who were forced to hurt each other, whereas you go to see Tom, and Jack, and dear Mary's brother Mr. Brown, hurt themselves ; and, God bless you, I hope you always will. So long as you do, this republic will never fail from the effeminacy of its young men.

The " gang " had got seats in the same car on the observation-train and were waiting for it to start.

" What were you doing with that Yale man

just now?" Hudson demanded of Randolph, as the latter joined the group on the platform.

"That was an old schoolmate of mine," answered Randolph, evasively.

."Oh, yes; and I suppose you were talking over your happy childhood days, with a bunch of bills in your fist. Fie! Johnny, you have been betting."

"You need n't put on airs. You were the first backslider of the lot," answered Randolph.

"I have n't put up a cent," protested Hudson.

"No, because you met a man who knew you and bet on tick. I heard you."

"A man who *did n't* know him, you mean," corrected Burleigh. "You are all a set of weak, reprehensible young men. I am ashamed of you. I depend upon you, at least, Hollis, my son, not to indulge in this wicked vice of betting."

"Yes," laughed Holworthy, "there must be some one left to float you home, if we lose."

"Now you mention it," Ned suggested, "perhaps you had better lend me an X now, in case we should get separated after the race. I want to prevent the spread of this athletic fever and the evils that follow in its train. I am afraid my governor may become too enthusiastic. If I go home to him again C. O. D. he will begin to take a real interest in seeing Harvard win, and I fear even a pecuniary one."

" This betting is indeed a deplorable evil," said Stoughton, solemnly, " in off years. Listen to me, my children. Two years ago I, even I, who now stand before you, was a reckless, ungodly Sophomore. I went——"

Just then the whistle blew, and Stoughton jumped for the car to get a front seat before the rest of the crowd. The long observation-train, a peculiar feature of the New London race, moved slowly out from the station on its way to the starting-point, four miles up the river. Then the cheering began, one car taking it up after another, the sharp quick cheers of the Yale men mingling with the slower full-mouthed three-times-three of Harvard. Every one is always in great spirits before the race begins,—it is different afterwards. They chaffed each other, and shouted, and laughed, and the enthusiastic choruses of " Here's to good old Yale, drink her down," were answered with the stirring, swelling cadences of " Fair Harvard."

When they got to the starting-point, of course the crews were not yet there. Across the river, however, at Red Top, the H. U. B. C. quarters, tall forms were seen entering the boat-house.

" Oh, how I wish I were like those chaps," sighed little Gray, who was already beginning to tremble with excitement. " What would n't I give to be able to pull an oar to-day."

" I have thought of it myself," said Burleigh; " but they would n't build the boat to suit my figure."

" The only thing I could do for the glory of Harvard was to try for coxswain," went on Gray, ruefully, " and they would n't have me."

" Was that the best you could do for Alma Mater?" said Holworthy. " What a pity you could n't succeed in putting such laurels on her brow ! "

" There, Gray, take that," chuckled Stough-ton ; " that is the time Pegasus fell down and got his neck stepped on."

" Are n't you ashamed of yourself, you hot-headed little poet," put in Hudson, gravely.

" How can you speak so thoughtlessly, even when sitting right beside Holworthy, the Superb? Can you, a member of the Oldest and Greatest take such a childish interest in.a paltry boat-race ? "

" You are forgetting all about the atmosphere, and the traditions, and all that sort of game," added Randolph. " What difference does it make to us whether we win or lose? Remember the true glories and blessings of our ancient University."

" For instance," drawled Rattleton, " whether we want to celebrate or console ourselves, we have all the royal crimson juices with which to do it, whereas those poor Elis can't find a blue drink to save their souls."

" Jove! I never thought of that. Glad I did n't go to Yale, are n't you, Gray?" exclaimed Stoughton.

" I don't believe the color of their booze troubles them much, as long as we pay for it," reasoned Burleigh. " Still, that is the proper spirit and the right way to look at these comparative collegiate advantages. Is n't it, Gray ? "

" If you chaps think you can get a rise out of

me," answered Gray to all this, " you are mistaken ; but for your own sakes you had better
not try to be so funny in public. As for you,
Hol, there is no use at all in your trying to play
the lofty indifferent. You are as much excited
as any man ; you look as if you were going to
row the whole thing yourself. I have been
watching you biting your knuckles and clench-
ing your fist and staring over at——"

He was interrupted by a great shout, and
everybody jumped to his feet. Out of the
boat-house opposite, came the long shell borne
by the Crimson eight. As they put it in the
water another shout went up, and a volley of
cheers, for at that moment the Yale crew shot
round the point from Gale's Ferry, with a beautiful snap and dash, and " let her run " in front
of the train. They were not kept waiting
long for the Cambridge men got quickly
into their boat and came swinging across,
showing but one crimson back until they
turned. There was perfect precision and splendid power in their sweep. There were five
men in the boat who had never pulled an oar
in the four-mile race, but they were all good
ones. Four had rowed on their class crews ;

the fifth, though a Freshman, had taken hold wonderfully, had a magnificent physique, and had come up with a good reputation from St. Paul's. And there was Dane Austin, L.S., at stroke, the hero of four 'Varsity races, and behind him at 7, old Billy Bender, the iron captain who, with all luck against him, had made a winning crew before, and certainly must have done so this year with such material. These two could surely "hit up" the stroke indefinitely, and in the middle of the boat towered Charlie Rivers, looking as if he could do all his own share and that of the three men behind him, if need might be.

Now both crews backed up to the starting boats, and off came the jerseys. They were right opposite the car. "Attention!" "Ready!" Rivers leaned forward and buried his blade alongside of Yale for his last chance. He had never won. Holworthy, bent almost double, gripping his chin in his hand, watched that statue. He could see no expression whatever in the sunburned profile and the motionless eye fixed on the neck before it. He wondered, —"Row!" He saw the oar bend so that his heart stopped for a moment in the fear that

the spruce would break. A mingled roar that
sounded like "YAYAVARD!" then silence so
that he could hear the clear, cool tones of
Varnum, the coxswain. He saw the mighty
shoulders heave back, and swing forward again
in one motion, the arms rigid as steel pistons.
Again, with not a movement of the arms.
"Row!" A third time, and this time the
great muscle leaped up and the arm was bent
until the oar butt touched the chest, then shot
out again like a flash, "Row! That's good ;
steady, now hold it." The roar burst out again,
and this time it sounded clear enough. HAR—
AR—VARD ! Holworthy took his eyes from
his chum and looked at the whole picture.
The little red coxswain was even with No. 3 in
the Yale boat ! It had been a perfect racing
start ; those three tremendous lightning strokes
had shot the Harvard eight nearly half a length
ahead of their rivals. There was no question
as to which were the stronger men, but strength
is the least thing of all that wins a boat-race.
After this first leap the Yale crew hung right
where it was, and would not fall clear of the
Crimson oars. At the mile flag Harvard had
not increased her lead perceptibly.

" That 's all right ; they 'll spurt in a minute,"
shouted Randolph.   So they did and gained a
little, at least so it seemed to the Crimson
wearers.

The shells were far out in the stream now,
and how slowly those two centipedes were
crawling! The two eights, that had dashed away
from the starting-point (which is close to the
bank), now seem to swing back and forth with
aggravating deliberation.

"There! There! now Yale 's coming up!"
"Not much, sir, look at that!" Since the
start that was the best struggle so far,—just
before the Navy-yard, and there was no question that this time Harvard had gained. At
the end of two miles she had a good length.

Again the Yale men spurt ; gaining? no, but
holding,—yes gaining,—there! Of course the
train has gone behind the island just at the
most exciting point. Everybody leans back
and tries to take a long breath. For a minute
nothing is heard but the chug, chug, chug of
the train.   Hark! the front cars are out, listen!
But that spontaneous indefinite yell may come
from the lungs of either, or both sides.   "Yale!
Yale ! YALE!" the two crews are even! Bow

and bow to the two and a half mile flag, and
the stroke is high now. But high as it is Dane
Austin is sending it higher, for Bender behind
him knows the vital importance of leading at
the three-mile flag, and has probably grunted
"hit her up." Slowly the Harvard shell pokes
ahead, a yard, two, a quarter of a length.
"Harvard! Harvard! Harvard!" The Crimson coxswain shows in the middle of the Yale
crew. "Can they hold it?" "Yale is spurting
like fury too." "No, the red coxswain is drop-
ping back." "They are even again." "No,
by Jove! Yale is ahead!" "YA-A-I-E!" Two
miles and three quarters and Yale is ahead for
the first time. Another desperate spurt and
the Harvard bow comes up even again, but
holds there less than a minute, and another
beautiful effort of the Yale crew sends their
boat farther ahead than before. The Cambridge men are not rowing as they were; they
are ragged; can they be weakening? There is
a break somewhere; seems to be in the middle.
The Blue coxswain is going ahead fast now.
Yes, there is a decided break right in the middle
of the Harvard crew. "Hullo! no wonder!
somebody is gone!" "What?" "No! Oh,

d—— it all, no, not No. 4?" " Man alive, you don't know who No. 4 is." " Can't be!" "Yes, but it is though." " Rivers, by —— Charlie Rivers!"

It was. Swaying irregularly, he was throwing himself back and forward all out of time.

" He is a passenger!" exclaimed a Yale man in the car. " It has been a fine race, but it will be a procession now. Those big men are no use in a boat."

" Hold on, my friend, look at that! If he *is* a passenger he is working his passage pretty hard still."

He did seem to gather himself for a moment, probably in response to a yell from the coxswain, and for a second the glimpse of open water between the boats was shut out by a Harvard spurt. It was no use. Yale drew away again faster than ever. Rivers was growing worse and worse. His head was loosening, but not falling yet; it was *snapping* back at the end of each stroke, a fault that showed he was still pulling hard, though all out of form and time.

Hollis Holworthy had not moved from his first position since the beginning of the race.

He had taken no part in, and paid no attention to the exclamations, shouts, and cheers around him. He had grown paler, that was all. Only now he muttered to himself, " He is too old an oar to pull himself out in the first two miles."

Jack Rattleton sat beside him. " He is doing it deliberately, Hol," he said softly, with a quivering lip.

" I don't believe it, Jack. You do him injustice. He has more grit and patience than that, and if he had not, he would not sacrifice the rest of the crew and the Crimson to his own madness. No, I can't make it out, but I don't believe that."

At the three and a quarter mile flag the New Haven men had a fast increasing stretch of clear water behind them and were going easily. How prettily they did row ! A winning crew with a safe lead always does.

And now began that most pathetic spectacle, the finish of a beaten eight-oared crew. Yet there was not one of their friends looking on who would not have given anything to have been pulling with them then. Where was that faultless form, that clock-like time, that glorious sweep, that at the start had raised an exultant

shout from every breast that bore the Crimson?
Much of the mighty strength was still there, but
pitifully divided against itself, and therefore fast
waning. The new men were, every one of them,
" rowing out of the boat," that is to say, swinging in a circular motion around the ends of
their oars, in their desperate efforts to pull their
hardest. The temptation to do this is generally
irresistible to a green man when behind. It
seems to him as if he can pull harder in this way,
and indeed it looks so to the unknowing ob-
server. Time and form are thrown overboard
in the wild struggle to row his heart out. Only
the two old veterans at 7 and 8 were still
swinging over the keel, not a hair's breadth
to starboard or port, coming forward steadily
and back with a simultaneous heave; their
backs straight, their chins in, two parallel un-
broken lines from hip to crown; their oars
taking the water cleanly and together, pulled
clear through, and flashing back at once with a
perfect feather. So evenly and smoothly did
they row that, to the untaught eye on the distant train, they might have seemed to be shirk-
ing; but to those on the yacht decks along the
course, the spread nostrils, clenched jaws, and

swollen veins told a very different story. An old Yale stroke, when his hat came down on deck again after the Yale crew had passed, let it lie where it fell as he gazed at the struggling tail-enders, and exclaimed, " Look at those two men in the stern. By gracious, is n't that grand ! " And Rivers, the third of the old guard, Rivers, who had been relied upon to brace the waist of the boat, who had before rowed that terrible fourth mile in a losing race and rowed it well; how was he finishing? Not an ounce of strength in his blade. He was still throwing his body to and fro with the others or nearly so, his head falling forward and back as he did so, and his oar moved ; but that was all. He was now being carried over the line by the crew he had ruined. He alone was doing nothing ; the others, though ragged, were still pulling desperately, using up the very last of their failing strength.

Through the buzzing in their ears they can faintly hear the guns, the whistles, and the roar of the crowd. Not for them, not for them. What difference does that make ? They may win, or at any rate they can lose like men. They may win, they may win. " Let her run."

Over the water from all sides come the cheers

and shouts of " Yale, Yale, Yale." Leave them, reader, if you so choose, they are beaten men ; go and rejoice with the victors who have rowed a splendid race and well deserve your congratu-lations. I always take a certain morbid interest myself in the nine heartbroken men who are quietly carried away in their launch as soon as possible after a race.

All over and lost in twenty minutes, the work and self-denial of seven months! The big Freshman has dropped his head on his knees and is sobbing like a baby ; of course it must be all his fault. Bill Bender is still grimly gripping his oar and looking straight before him ; that back is bent now, but the jaw is still set, the eyes flashing, and through his teeth he registers a vow to come back to the Law School and get at 'em again. Varnum, the coxswain, is as pale as the rest ; he has rowed every stroke of that race without the savage comfort of the physical torture ; he has seen what the others could not —the Blue coxswain going farther and farther ahead, and he powerless to help his straining men. They all hold on to something or clasp their knees tightly—to faint or fall over would be a grand-stand play.

Nevertheless that was what Charles Rivers did. He swayed for a moment, grasped blindly at the side of the shell, and fell back unconscious in the lap of the man behind him. And then, for the first time, No. 3 saw that the bottom of the boat was red with blood. *Rivers had broken his sliding-seat before the two mile flag was reached, and had rowed the last half of the race sliding back and forth on the sharp steel tracks that cut into him at every stroke.**

Before the observation-train had fairly stopped Holworthy leaped from it and dashed for the river bank followed by Rattleton. As they passed one of the cars they both recognized a girl with a blue flag. Holworthy said something that Jack did not hear; the former did not notice that the girl's face was deadly pale and the blue flag motionless in her hand, but the latter did.

"There is no use in our following them," said Burleigh. "They won't be allowed to talk to the crew even if they get out to the float." Therein he was quite right; before the two could get a boat to go out to the Harvard float

---

* There is no fiction about this. It was done by a Harvard oarsman.

at the finish, they saw the men helped out of the shell and onto the University launch. They saw Rivers carried aboard. Then the launch steamed quickly up the river, towing the empty shell.

" Hullo, there is my uncle's boat," exclaimed Rattleton, pointing to a big schooner. " I am going aboard her. You go back to New London and get a trap, and I 'll meet you at the ferry."

Holworthy ran back towards the town. On the way he met the others, who stopped him to hear what was up.

" I don't know," he replied. " He is completely gone. I am going up to the quarters. You fellows must n't come. They won't allow a crowd there."

" Where is Jack? "

" Gone aboard his uncle's yacht. Rather think he has gone to ask for an invitation for Charlie. Hope so."

" Is n't there anything we can do? "

" Not a thing. Don't try to see him, please; you probably won't have a chance to, anyway."

" You won't dine with us then? "　·

" Can't possibly."

" Well then, good-bye, old man. We 'll all

come back together next year and see them win."

"Good-bye. Write to a fellow once in a while and let me know how you are all getting on in the world."

"Good-bye." "Good-bye." "Good luck to you." "Thank heaven we have all been at Harvard anyway." This last for the benefit of a knot of radiant men who pushed by, with violets in their button-holes, and who looked back and laughed good-naturedly.

So "the gang" separated, and so separate constantly, after this battle, not knowing when they will ever meet again, men who have lived together four years and have become the closest friends that live.

Half an hour later Holworthy and Rattleton in a buggy were on their way to Red Top. All sorts of rumors had already spread about No. 4 in the Harvard boat, and they were really relieved to find, on arriving at the quarters, that Rivers was nowhere near death's door, not even permanently injured. But the great, stalwart, glorious man was weak and limp as an invalid girl. As soon as possible they got him away from the gloomy group at the quarters, and took him aboard the cruiser of Rattleton's uncle for perfect rest and sparkling blue water.

There they kept him prisoner for two weeks, though before he had fairly got back his strength, he began chafing to get to work. When at last they let him go, he buckled down to his desk, as he had to his oar, and kept at it until, at the end of the summer, a short vacation was forced on him.

.   .   .   .

The following cablegram, received by " Herr Holz Holvordy," at St. Moritz, explains itself :

NEWPORT, Sept. 5.

She is mine.   Hurrah.   Be my best man.

RIVERS.

At the wedding every one remarked what a handsome couple they were, and how well suited to each other.   Holworthy of course was best man.   The ushers were Messrs. Bender, Burleigh, Gray, Hudson, Randolph, and Stoughton. Jack Rattleton happened to be abroad at the time.

THE END.

www.ingramcontent.com/pod-product-compliance
Lightning Source LLC
Chambersburg PA
CBHW060530030726
47498CB00004B/1143